Wolves of Cold Creek

Scarlett's

Tail

Brittany Putzer

This is for those suffering in a prison of darkness. Your happily ever after is but a moment away...

Trigger Warning

Scarlett's Tail is a dark wolf-shifter romance and contains scenes that may be upsetting for some readers. The content includes triggers such as (but not limited to): age-gap sex and foreplay, murder, death, profanity, violence, graphic sexual activities, demanding alpha men, needy headstrong women, witchcraft, guardian angels, and sexual assault.

CONTENTS

Scarlett

The Fangs

My heart pounds in my ears as my feet beat against the cold concrete.

"What are you idiots doing just standing there? Somebody, grab her!"

The pedestrians gawk as I rush by, but with one look at my dingy attire, their pity-filled expressions face forward. And I might as well be invisible. The thick raindrops hammer against my skin as I race away from the grocery store with two large men trailing behind me—their screams directed at my back.

I duck inside the dark alleyway and leap on top of a metallic dumpster. From there, I grip the slick fire escape and drag myself onto the roof. I gasp for oxygen, trying to fill my burning lungs before they're exerted for a second time—*today.* Once my breathing has somewhat normalized, I peek at the security guards while they scratch their heads and curse loudly. They scan the cramped space for another moment, then report in their earpieces that I escaped their grasps. *Again.*

I snicker to myself as I comb my hands through my crimson hair. *I won't go hungry tonight.*

Suddenly, there is a warm body standing behind me. Fingertips dance along my neck before a metallic object glides towards my throat. "Well, look who's running from the pigs again."

"Aren't you tired of getting your ass whooped, Tanner?"

"Scarlett, admit it. I have you pinned and there is no escaping. Surrender to me."

"In your dreams." I slam my elbow into his stomach while I tuck and roll. Even with my quick countermove, he manages to slice my arm, but it's better than my neck. "Hey, asshole! That's going to leave a scar!"

Tanner coughs in the background as I stomp off towards the Warehouse. *I'm such an idiot.* I can't believe I took that moment to gloat. I'm getting rusty, but I vow to never let that happen again.

As I reach my destination, my boots skid to a stop near an icy patch. My clenched fist pounds on the Warehouse door. While it echoes, I rub my hands together and watch the fog escape my lips. *Damn! Hurry up and answer the door!*

A sudden clang causes me to leap and twist. I drop my makeshift ninja stance once I realize there's no threat—only dumpster fires offering bright warmth to the many homeless cloaked figures.

"What do you have for me tonight, Scarlett?" I respond by pulling out two cans of Chef Boyardee and tossing them to the older man at the door. "Do you really think *that* will gain you entrance? Two cans?"

"Come on, Stan! I had to run two miles in the freezing rain for those cans."

"How about you keep me warm tonight, sugar? Then we can call it even, and I'll let you in."

I'm used to these jerks. They think that just because I'm young and easy on the eyes, I'll service their limp dicks for extras.

Well, fuck them. I snatch my cans and stalk off with my middle finger flying for all to see.

"Stan, let her in." Tanner throws the doorman four cans. "You're a sick bastard. If she's keeping anybody warm tonight, it'll be somebody her own age. I mean, come on! She could be your grandkid." He chuckles as he guides me inside.

"I was handling him, Tanner. I didn't need you standing up for me."

"I was only trying to help."

"Yeah, after you tried to slice my throat for *my* cans? Just stay the hell away from me." I stomp towards a pile of cardboard. Although nobody can stake a claim on spots, this one's my favorite. It's close to the heater *and* the exit. Once I settle on the floor, I rub my numb fingers and blow hot air on the tips.

"I saved this spot for you." I try not to show the shock in my emerald eyes as the tiny voice squeaks behind me.

"Sara, I told you it wasn't safe here. Why didn't you go back to the orphanage or the fire station this morning?"

"I don't want to go back there without you. I miss you."

The tiny blonde curls into my lap like a guilt-ridden puppy. I grumble before stroking her hair and kissing her forehead. "I'm sorry, sweetie, but you can't stay here."

"Why can't you go back with me. Don't you love me anymore?"

My heart squeezes at the sadness dripping from her words. I pinch my eyes shut and scream at myself internally: *Do not cry. Stay strong.* "I already told you... I'm too old for the orphanage."

"You *just* turned eighteen. Can't they make an exception? They didn't have to kick you out on your birthday."

"Times are tough, and they had to make room for more needy children. So they don't end up here, stealing and lying to survive."

I feel her slow, even breathing and realize she's asleep. This sweet girl has *no* idea how rough this place is. *Especially* for a woman. And I don't intend on her *ever* finding out.

I met Sara when she was dropped off at St. Paul's. The dirty ragamuffin was screaming and crying as she begged her mother to come back. I comforted her as best I could and became a sort of surrogate maternal figure, wiping her tears and making sure she had enough to eat. But once the orphanage kicked me out, Sara was on her own and sneaking passed the night guard when he drifted off to sleep. No one came looking for her, because it was one less mouth to feed. But I won't let her live on the streets and end up like her mother. A shiver runs through me at the memory of the last time I saw that woman.

It was the first week I meandered the streets of Carson City. I was cold and hungry. But it was hard to find a compassionate heart in the decaying metropolis. That night, I spent four hours begging for loose change. Once I mustered enough, I bought a cheeseburger and scarfed it down. When I left the restaurant, I observed two men beating a homeless person before they stole a baggie from her pocket. I ran over to help, but I was shell-shocked when I realized it was Sara's mother. Thankfully, the men already got what they wanted and realized it wasn't worth the fight when I approached. But it was too late for the woman at my feet. I ran my hand over

4

her bruised face and took in the tiny pricks on her arms. The scene brought me to my knees, and I wept over her lifeless form, though not for her. No, my heart broke for her innocent daughter, who dreamed of one day locating her mother when she was finally old enough to leave the orphanage. It wasn't long before a tall dark-haired man discovered my disheveled figure crouched over the corpse… and collected me without a word.

That's when I met Spike, and my world became grimmer. I don't know why he chose to take me in that night, because he is anything but compassionate. He is middle-aged and the leader of the city gang known as the Fangs. They took me in and showed me how to survive on the crumbling streets. And they alone hold the power in the Warehouse and most of the city. If you want to survive, this is the group to fall into.

Admittedly, I don't consider myself a true member. Don't get me wrong, I appreciate everything they've taught me, because I don't think I would have survived without their assistance. But I am a loner. I have to be. I've had enough pain in my short existence, without adding more. When I was three years old, I was dropped off at the orphanage by a police officer who found me wandering the woods near Cold Creek. Consequently, I couldn't communicate well, and they weren't able to learn where I came from or who I was. The other kids called me Scarlett because of my red hair, and the name stuck.

No middle name. No last name. No family.

Sara stirs in my lap and whimpers. I softly hum the tune of "Hush, Little Baby" to her, and she wiggles before she relaxes.

"What have you eaten today?" I don't need to crane my neck to know who is looming over me with a stern expression.

"I've eaten."

"Why do you insist on lying to me, Little Wolf?" I am blessed with agility and a keen sense of hearing, hence his pet name for me. Little Wolf. And he is the *only* one permitted to use it. When I remain silent, he kicks my foot, looking to elicit a response.

"I answered you already, Spike."

He drops a sandwich into my lap while glaring. "If you lie to me again, I will force you to sleep outside in the freezing sleet."

I can't stand that he believes he owns me. I toss the sandwich back. As a result, Sara rubs her eyes. "Is it morning already?" Her yawn is wide, and my heart melts as her gaze is still painted by dreams.

"Scarlett, take your friend upstairs to the loft. She doesn't belong down here."

"I'm watching over her. She is fine. And I'll bring her back in a few hours."

"It wasn't a request. Now pick her up, or I'll have somebody else grab her." The unpleasant edge to his command makes me leap to my feet with the small girl still cradled in my arms. But the sudden movement causes my vision to blur, and I sway. Spike catches my waist before I tumble. "You are going to kill yourself... *and her.* Now get your ass up those stairs."

Spike snatches Sara before he sets her on the ground. Then he grabs my elbow and tugs me towards the staircase. I grumble as I obey, following her to the second floor. Once we cross the threshold, an involuntary moan escapes my lips as the warmth of the room crawls up my frozen toes. This area is off-limits because it's Spike's personal living quarters. The only time you are allowed up here is if you are keeping his bed hot for the night. I glance around at the small but cozy space. It has a king bed, a bathroom, a kitchen, and a decent-size common room.

Sara squeals as she plops on the leather couch and wraps an enormous fleece blanket around her tiny shoulders. "This place is *amazing*! Who would have thought it would be attached to that dump?"

"Don't get too comfortable, okay. We are going back to the orphanage in a few hours."

Spike kneels in front of Sara with narrowed eyes. "Listen here, little girl. I better not see you in *my* warehouse again. This is not a place for children. You could get hurt or go missing."

Sara swallows while her pupils grow wide. Slowly, she pivots and her icy eyes bore into mine before filling with tears. "But then I will never see Scarlett again."

Spike snatches her trembling chin and forces her to look away from me. "I don't give a shit. If I see you here again, I will make Scarlett disappear from your life. So, either way, you are going to lose her." His words send chills down my spine. Spike is known for both his anger and his ability to make individuals vanish. Although he allows me to banter with him, I know my limits. "Now you will sit here, watch TV, and fall asleep."

Sara only nods as he hands her the remote. Her tears silently slide down her cheeks and my heart aches.

Before I can comfort her, Spike pulls me into his room and slams the door. "What were you thinking, bringing her here?"

"Sara was here when I came in. I would never *bring* her here."

He pivots on his heels and marches out the door with a look that could kill. I swallow, glad that his anger is no longer focused on me. Once his footsteps are silent, I glance around the bare walls of his bedroom. His choice in decor doesn't give much away. There is only one photo on his dresser—it's of him and another man who looks to be related to him.

I run my hand over the soft cotton comforter and moan. How long has it been since I've slept in an actual bed? I peek into his bathroom and smile at the sparkling white tile. When my gaze lands on the mirror, I cringe. There are dark circles under my bright-green eyes, while crimson strands plaster my dirty skin. I trail my finger over the wound Tanner inflicted and wince. When my pupils meet in my reflection, I attempt to stare into my own soul and *will* my forgotten past to come forward.

Who are you really, Scarlett? Where did you come from? Who are your parents?

The longer I stare, the more distorted my vision becomes. After a few minutes, I blink and a warm tear escapes while reality sets in. I am a nobody. A meaningless lifeform.

Suddenly, the bedroom door clicks, and I pivot to discover Spike. My gaze trails over his rolled-up sleeves and cut knuckles. I purse my lips, wondering whose blood is decorating his jeans and sweater, but I know better than to ask questions when it comes to his brutality. There is a fire burning in his eyes as they land on me. "I'm not in the mood for your bullshit. I'm going to ask you one last time. Have you eaten today?" His rage-laced words slap me across the face, and I have to look away.

"No, I haven't. I gave up my meal at the door because Stan asked for it."

"Well, Stan will *never* demand food from you again. Or anybody else, for that matter." He tosses a glint of silver covered in crimson onto the bathroom counter. I jump before realizing it's Stan's high school ring—the one that he always wears. *Shit.* "Stan's permanent residence is now in a body bag six feet underground." Spike brushes past me while yanking his sweater over his head. For a middle-aged man, he is easy on the eyes, with his natural tan and thick muscles. "Go to the kitchen and make yourself something to eat, before you fall over again."

"I never fell over. I just lost my balance."

"Are you *trying* to test my patience?" His words bounce off the bathroom surfaces, and I pale. He easily closes the gap between us, pinning me to the wall with his overheated body. "You have forgotten your place, Scarlett, and I think it's about time you remembered."

"I'm sorry, Spike. I'll go and make something to eat. Do *you* want something?"

He doesn't move to let me by. "Do you value that little girl?"

"You know I do."

"Well, I *thought* you did. But that mouth of yours will get her sleeping next to Stan. Do I make myself clear?"

"Yes, sir."

He watches me carefully, and just when I think he has more to say, he steps aside. I let out a breath and scurry past him with my tail between my legs. Once in the kitchen, I shuffle around the contents of his fridge before squealing with delight at its treasures. I cook eggs, bacon, and biscuits.

"It looks like you've made quite the feast, Little Wolf."

We sit at the table, and I attempt to *not* scarf down my meal as my stomach demands more. I feel Spike's watchful gaze but that doesn't deter my hunger. "This is very good." I peer up with arched brows. Spike never verbalizes his approval. "Don't look at me like that, girl. I just gave you a compliment. What do you say in return?"

"Thank you."

"Do you remember anything about your parents or your past?"

9

It's an odd turn in conversation.

"I have already told you… no."

He rubs his stubble. "What if I offer you a *new* start? Why don't you marry one of the members and let them take care of you? How about Tanner? You two seem to hang out a lot."

I blink. *Where is this coming from?* "I appreciate the thought, but I'm only eighteen years old and I have *no* interest in marriage." I rub the gash on my arm. "Or in Tanner."

"You are an adult now. Surely you have thought about starting your own family?"

"No, it hasn't crossed my mind. You know, between the scrounging for food and fighting to stay alive in this godforsaken city, I just haven't had the time."

"Watch that sarcasm," he warns before continuing. "You are to attend a meeting with me tomorrow night, with the others. It's about time you pledge yourself to the group and learn our ways." He stands. "Once you are officially a member, we can match you and then you will never have to worry about food again."

His words paralyze me. "No, I can't. I'm not ready for that."

"It's funny how you *assume* you have a choice in the matter. While you are living in my town, you will abide by my will. Now clean up, shower, and come to bed." He strides out of the room without a backwards glance.

The scalding water melts my chilled frame. I rest my forehead on the tile while the warmth massages my achy muscles. Knowing what awaits me beyond those doors, I remain in the protective steam for as long as I can. Spike never invites anybody to the loft, especially at night. I know why I'm here. He wants my body.

As the water turns cold, I finally decide to leave the safety of the shower stall. Swiping my palm across the foggy mirror, I remind my reflection that I'm lucky, considering Spike is kind and *mostly* generous with this process. It could be worse.

I shudder as I recall the first night I stayed in the Warehouse, and I saw a woman leave his loft. Her lip was swollen, and she donned a black eye.

I take in a deep breath. I must become another person when I'm with him. I won't be Scarlett. I will be Sally. Sally, the slut who doesn't mind having sex with a man for a warm meal, a bed, and protection. I cringe. A man old enough to be my father.

I open the bathroom door and stare into his hungry gaze. He runs his hand over my face as he takes in my naked body. "Do you remember what I expect of you?"

"Yes, I do."

"And you agree to this?"

I swallow and nod. Sally is here and reporting for duty, while Scarlett huddles in the corner.

"Good. Now prove to me how grateful you are for everything I have given to you." We lock eyes as he removes his clothes and tosses them aside. "Get on your knees."

I do as I'm told and take another deep breath, before sucking his length into my mouth. The salty, warm liquid flows down my throat as his groans reverberate off the walls. He wraps my hair around his hand and thrusts into my throat, obstructing my airway. But I continue to do his bidding.

"You know this is where you *belong*. On your knees, in front of me." His words are labored and his thrusts more urgent. My eyes water as his member throbs. To speed him along, I gently squeeze his testicles, and I'm rewarded with a grunt while he releases his load. He waits until I swallow every drop before he frees my hair. "Stand up."

He guides his fingertips through my tousled locks and pauses at the back of my scalp. He massages it tenderly before he shoves my lips against his. His mouth covers mine, then he slips his tongue inside and claims me. His palms caress my body, lingering on my breasts so he can squeeze my nipples until they are forced to form hard peaks. Slowly, he drags his tongue over each one, suckling at the sensitive flesh. And I'm lost to my alter ego, playing along with reciprocated moans.

"You like that, don't you?" He grins against my tender neck as he slips his finger inside my core and twirls. At the sudden insertion, I clench—and Sally is pushed back while I'm shoved forward. "The more you struggle, the more painful it will be," he purrs as he nips my earlobe.

He then shoves me against the bed before he lifts me into a sitting position. His eyes never leave mine as he runs his wet finger across my lips.

"Taste yourself." I draw his digit into my mouth. The salty sweetness glides down my throat. "Now it's my turn to have a taste." Spike trails impassioned kisses all the way to my core, where he slams his tongue inside and flicks, as his hand moves along my sex. I clench again, not wanting to experience this assault on my senses. "Scarlett, just relax and enjoy my *gift*."

I lean my head onto the pillow and arch my back, as Sally takes over again and Scarlett covers her ears.

"Good girl. Now scream my name for everybody to hear." He

intensifies his touch while using his knuckles to tweak my nipples. The battle over ignoring him versus allowing my body to react is getting harder to win, as my brain is clouded by his forced pleasure. "You know I won't stop until I accomplish what I came to do for you."

His meaning washes over my body, and my hands clench the bedsheets as my climax inches closer. Spike stops abruptly and observes my heavy respirations.

"Say it." My vision is glazed over with desire, and I loathe myself. He runs his hand through my fuzz to my sex. "Say it, and I will give you your release."

The heat from his hand makes me whimper. "I can do it myself."

"Always so tenacious." He pins my arms above my head. "You know I won't let you. So, just say what I want to hear." He kisses my neck, waiting for the declaration to leave my mouth. When I don't give him what he wants, he bites my nipples until I cry out as I near my breaking point.

Damn it, Scarlett, just say it, Sally screams. The words are forming but refuse to leave the tip of my tongue.

Spike touches every part of me *but* where I need it most. *I know* he will keep this up all night if he has to. And *he knows* I will eventually become weak and give in to his dirty tricks.

Suddenly, his tongue flicks my clit and I arch with a hiss.

"*I* know you want this. *You* know you want this. Just give in." He slips two fingers inside and moves in and out while he blows warm air on my overly sensitive parts.

I squirm, but he holds me in place. "Please," I whimper.

"Please, what?"

A warm tear falls, followed by my resolve. "Please *help* me, Spike. I need you."

He finally allows me to explode beneath him, and I scream out his name for everybody to hear. Then he kisses me deeply, mingling my juices with his own. "You're ready for me, *so* ready." He slides inside me before he pounds roughly, grunting until he warms my insides with his quick release. "Go clean yourself up."

I, again, do as I'm told because I have *no* way out. Because my life is in his hands. My worthless, insufferable life.

Sable

Taken Mate

"Sky, please, I can't eat another bite."

"Yes, you can! And you *will!* I need these dishes taste-tested for my catering event tomorrow."

"Do you want your big brother to gain ten pounds? Come on! Don't you have enough employees at the restaurant to help you out?"

"They have already tried them." She presents her signature baby sister pout. "You are my *only* hope."

"Fine. One more entrée. Then I'm done."

Sky grins as she slides over a heavily gravied meat dish. My keen wolf senses pick up the steak before my knife slices through it. My taste buds pop as the perfect melody of salt and pepper dance in my mouth. "This is the one you should serve."

"Are you sure, Sable?"

I push back my chair before my expanding ass has time to splinter it. I brush off the crumbs and meet her expectant gaze. "*Skylar*, seriously. I gave you my answer. Stop looking at me like that! I'm done and going back home." I kiss the top of her head. "Good night."

"But, Sable, you haven't even tried my penis-shaped sugar cookies!" She cries at my departing back. I lift my hand, not daring to look her way again. My sister was the middle child and rarely ever told *no*.

"Hello, hot stuff."

I smirk at the golden goddess manning the hostess stand. "Hey, Carly."

I give her a quick hug and gesture behind me. "Be careful. She is on the prowl, trying to shove dicks in my mouth and calling it dessert."

"Yeah, she is getting a jump start on Valentine's Day prep, and the college-age clientele can't resist a good phallic-themed baked good. Plus, those cookies actually taste better than the real thing." She winks. "Don't you worry your pretty little head about Sky. I'll calm her down."

"Oh, I have no doubt. I'm sure you have your *ways*."

Those two have a curious relationship. Like me, Sky is a shifter, but Carly is only human. Though, it seems they developed a complex bond in college. They know each other's dirty little secrets and have spent many experimental nights under the covers.

"Sable?" I cringe as my sister's demanding, high-pitched voice blares down the hall.

"Well, that's my cue. See you later." I take off to the nearest exit while I throw over my shoulder, "Good luck!"

Once the night air hits me, I stretch out. The fresh scent of pine awakens my nerve endings, and my wolf itches to run free in the forest. I quickly turn the corner towards the dark alley behind my sister's restaurant and shed my restrictive clothing. Then my fur rips through my pores, and I howl at the moon before galloping into the velvety night. The air is chilled, but my winter coat does its job. The leaves crunch as my claws tear through them, eager to get to my next destination. The rhythmic motion relaxes me and allows my wolf's thoughts to take over. That's when *she* comes to mind. My beautiful Maya.

She was stolen from our territory when she was just a little pup. We searched for years, with no luck. The pack feared the worst. But my wolf never gave up hope. He constantly sniffs her out whenever he can, refusing to let go of the one true mate Luna bestowed upon him, before greedily taking her away from us. Her wild white hair and soft amber eyes haunt my dreams, beckoning me to find her.

Suddenly, something leaps from the darkness. I dodge it, sliding to a stop and baring my teeth at the shadow. My nose twitches. I jump onto the fur ball, and we wrestle among the dirt and leaves. I lock my jaw around its neck, and my opponent cowers. Then I shift and laugh. "Did you really think you could surprise me?"

"Admit it, I almost had you. I smelled your fear."

"That was pure instinct, little brother." I collect him in a tight grip and rub my knuckles over his hair. "You'll never best me, Aspen."

He shoves me off before he fixes his tangled mess. "Mark my words, one day I will."

"Yeah, only in your dreams."

"Is Sky coming?"

I look past him and shake my head. "No, she is still working." Then I wrap an arm around his neck and squeeze. "Mom said you had a date tonight."

"Shut up."

I guide him towards our cave and continue to pester him. "How did it go? Wait, let me guess: she realized how *boring* you were before the date even began."

"Ha-ha-ha. Very funny. Says the guy who hasn't had a date in over a year. You're just jealous."

"No, I'm smart. I stay the hell away from all the crazies."

Aspen pulls back and snorts. "I always knew you liked men better anyway."

I blink at him as he spins on his heel and enters the house. When did he grow a pair of balls? Then I leap forward, taking him to the ground again.

"If you break another lamp, I'll take it out on your hides."

I tickle Aspen until his face is red. "Is this better, Mom?"

"If you make him pee on the rug again, I'll force your wolf to lick it up."

I stop, not wanting the punishment she'd have no qualms about dishing out. I may be a grown twenty-five-year-old, but my mother always follows through with her threats. Aspen catches his breath before he submits for a second time today. I follow my mom into the kitchen and watch as she stirs her famous stew. It's loaded with meat, potatoes, carrots, and onion. "Did your sister feed you?"

"Sorry, Mom. She forced me to try some new dishes. Trust me, I'd rather have your stew."

"Oh, well, there's always leftovers." I nod in response, grab a beer from the fridge, and settle at the table to sip it. "So, I heard Bridgett is back in town," my mom sings.

I arch a brow at her mention of another pack's unclaimed female. "And?"

"Well, I was hoping you two could get together."

"Mom."

"I'm serious, Sable."

"I appreciate you looking out for me, but I can find my own dates. *When I'm ready.*"

She pulls out the chair next to me. "One kiss, that's all I'm asking."

I groan as I lean back. Shifters are assigned a mate by the goddess, Luna. And the only way to tell if you are fated is to kiss. Supposedly, when your lips touch, you come in your pants—or at least that's how everybody makes it sound. It's ridiculous. I knew Maya was my mate the moment she looked into my eyes. It was a warm sensation that spread throughout my body and screamed *home*. But she has been gone for over a decade. I swirl my beverage around in thought. "Fine," I huff out.

"Really? Great! I asked her to stop by tomorrow afternoon, during your normal lunch break."

Yeah, *great*. As if running a mechanic shop wasn't hard enough. Although I love being my own boss, there's a lot to it. And now I'll have to entertain Bridgett at my place of business. "I'm only agreeing to one kiss. That's it. Then you and Dad will get *off* my back."

She pecks my cheek. "No promises, dear. But I'll at least hold off for a few months." She pinches my face to tug away my frown. "It's only because I love you and want to see you happy. Plus, I demand grandpups."

I rub my cheek before clasping on to Aspen's wrist as he *attempts* to tiptoe towards the stew unnoticed. "Why don't you guys just give up on me and help Aspen find a good bitch?"

My brother groans as Mom attacks him next with a bombardment of questions about his most recent *special friend*. I slip past them to call it a night. As much as I would love to sink my canines into a perky pair of breasts, my wolf won't listen. He wants what he wants. And nobody comes close to Maya.

Scarlett

The Meadow

"Keep your eyes closed and stay behind me."

"Who's coming?"

My pupils widen as a snarl vibrates the trees. Begging him to hold me in the safety of his arms, I yank at the man's legs as he stands in front of me.

"Don't be frightened. I'll protect you. I promise."

My lip quivers but I hold back my sob. There is nothing to fear. I squeeze my lids shut, and as an extra precaution, I shove my fingers into my ears. Muffled voices blare and a heated fight breaks out at my feet. I squeak but do as I'm told. My protector wraps his arms around me and runs into the darkness. Assuming it is safe again, I open my eyes and move my fingertips to his neck. "You're bleeding."

"I'll be fine. Remember to keep your—"

We are knocked to the ground and tumble for what feels like hours.

My protector cradles me, taking the brunt of the fall. But now his body is crushing my much smaller frame. I can't breathe. And just when I start to panic, the weight is lifted and tossed aside like a rag doll. I watch with wide eyes as crimson oozes from my protector's head before it pools at my feet. I wiggle my toes, surprised by the warmth. Then I reach down to tap the liquid. As my hand is coated with the tacky substance, there is an earth-shattering howl that rattles my soul.

I start with a yelp, rubbing my eyes and inspecting my fingertips. Damn dream…

I glare at Spike's draped arm as it rests on my hip. "Little Wolf?" he mumbles against his pillow. "Did you have another nightmare?"

"No, go back to sleep."

His fingers dig into my waist and I squeal. "What did I say about lying?" Spike trails kisses along my neck, turning me towards him in the process. "Do you want me to help you forget?" he purrs. "I can offer a pleasurable distraction."

"You got what was required. You won't get any more out of me." I shove him and scurry away from the bed before he can force himself on top of me. I've been humiliated enough for today. I pad to the living room and cuddle with Sara as she watches *SpongeBob*. We snuggle under her blanket and zone out as we take comfort in each other's presence.

Sara is unusually quiet as we walk in the crisp morning air. Once the orphanage comes into view, she squeezes my hand. "Please don't make me go. I won't be a problem… *I promise.* We can live together and help each other."

I take in a steadying breath, then kneel in front of her. "I'll come back for you as soon as I get on my own two feet. *I promise.* Cross my heart and hope to die."

Sara wraps her arms around my neck. "If you break that promise, I'll be mad at you for the rest of my life."

"Behave and stay here where it's safe, okay. If I have to keep on worrying about your wellbeing, I can't prepare for your arrival."

Sara nods as she pulls away. I escort her up the stone staircase leading to the front door, and my heart feels like it's breaking.

This is why you don't get attached, I scream at myself. I observe Sara dragging her feet through the entrance, and I offer a final wave once they pull her back into safety.

"Goodbye, Sara," I whisper as she disappears inside. Then I kick at the gravel walkway as I pivot on my heel. This must be goodbye. Because I won't let Spike get his claws on the one thing that matters most to me.

"Why the long face?"

"Are you following me, Tanner?"

"The boss wanted to ensure your friend made it back home." I ignore him, shoving my hands deep into my pockets as a cold wind tosses my hair. "And he wanted to ensure you didn't run for the hills before our gathering tonight at the meadow."

"Like I have any choice in the matter. Where the hell does he think I'll go?"

Tanner taps my shoulder with his. "You know, you're lucky he's been so patient with you. Why *you're* his favorite, I'll never understand."

"I'm not his favorite. He treats me the same as everybody else."

"He took you into the loft last night," Tanner draws out.

"I didn't have a choice."

"And he gave you a hot meal, a shower, and a warm bed to sleep in. I'm sure he pulled your leg really hard for that too."

"He also demanded I leave Sara alone, or he would kill her. Oh, and then he told me I needed to join his stupid group and marry one of his goons."

"We aren't all stupid."

"Pfft. Stop trying to convince yourself."

Our stroll around the city is accompanied by silence. Tanner is one of the better guys. He doesn't pressure me to do anything with him, never spits harsh words in my direction, and at times, acts like a friend. As the sun fades, so does my optimism for tonight's gathering. Dread clutches my throat at the thought of joining the Fangs.

"Well, here we are. What do you think?" Tanner asks.

I jump out of the van and stride into the large field. In the center is a burning bonfire, its embers flickering into the night sky. I crane my neck and watch in awe as the scene gives the illusion of long talons grasping for the full moon. Even though this is my first time here, I can't help but feel a sense of familiarity. An almost calming sensation washes over me. "Where are we?"

"Some ancient Native American burial ground. The tradition is: every year, on this exact day and time, the Fangs gather their new members in this precise location. The spirits of these lands are said to be active, and they offer strength to those who assemble in their presence."

"Do you actually believe in that crap?"

"Come on. You can't tell me you don't feel *something* different here. Maybe something special?"

I take in the crisp air and allow the scent of the land to register. This place does feel special, but I don't think *ghosts* have anything to do with it.

"Well, there's the *princess*." A tall, inked man stalks over. "The boss's little pet." From the cadence of Freddy's speech, I assume his cup isn't filled with fruit punch. When he steps into my personal bubble, I recoil at the stench. "Aw, what? Does her highness not like me standing too close to her? Afraid I may wrap my hands around that perfect little neck and—"

"Enough, Freddy. Back off." I square my shoulders.

"Or what?" His growl shakes me to my very core, but I shove him hard in the chest, spilling his beverage onto the grass. Feet shuffle around us as everybody waits for the inevitable fight.

"Now, now, children. Is this any way for a family to behave? Knock it off, before Daddy beats some sense into you both," Spike warns as he parts the group.

"Sorry, boss." Freddy backs off, glaring at me in the process.

"It won't happen again," I push out.

"What have I told you about lying to me, Little Wolf?"

The guys snicker at my nickname, which doesn't help my less-than-stellar mood. "I will try to *not* kick his ass while you're watching. Better?"

"Let's take a walk." I stroll beside him while wrapping my arms across my chest, glad the large fire is near to battle the wind's intermittent caress. "Tanner informed me that you escorted your friend back home. How is she doing?"

Experience tells me that he doesn't give a shit about how Sara is *actually* doing. He is just bringing her up to reiterate his threat. I must keep up my end of the deal, or her life will be that much shorter. In other words, my participation tonight is what will solidify her safety. "I'm sure she'll live a long, happy life."

"I'm pleased to hear it." He waves towards tables laden with food and beverages. "Tonight, we are celebrating, so feel free to eat and drink to your heart's content. The festivities will begin soon."

The smoky scent of barbecue has drool pooling in the crevices of my mouth. Tanner tosses a paper plate to me like a frisbee. "Stay away from the beans. The steaks are the best. They marinade them with this awesome sauce and cook them just enough to where they're still bloody in the center." He continues to guide me through each delicacy before we sit, while I try to not let Freddy's continuous glare ruin my dinner.

Everything smells so good: steak, baked potatoes, baked beans, corn on the cob, asparagus. I dig in as I attempt to pace myself, dabbing at my cheek as blood drips down. Tanner is right; the steak is perfect. Where do the Fangs get the funds for such an extravagant spread? And why couldn't every day be like this?

After we eat, the group gathers around the flames, forming a circle. The crackling of the logs and welcoming warmth eases my tension. Once everyone is settled, Spike clears his throat from beside me and addresses the group. "Welcome to our annual ancestral banquet." He brings a crystal-clear glass of red liquid to his lips and takes a swig. "This ceremonial wine symbolizes the blood that has been sacrificed for us by our past members, while also reminding us of the inevitable loss we are to face in the coming days. Luna, we thank and praise you for your blessings."

Wait, what did he say? What the fuck was in that drink?

Next, he passes the chalice to me with an encouraging yet forceful nod. I sniff the contents before bringing it to my lips. Does Spike realize I'm not old enough to drink alcohol? Or is underaged drinking not against his "gang" code?

The red fluid coats my throat as it glides down and warms its way to my chest. I pass it to Tanner, and he does the same with less hesitation. This process continues until everybody has partaken in the gesture. By the time the cup makes it back to Spike, he downs the rest and pitches the glass into the inferno. I leap as gold sparks burst into the air. Then music booms, setting everybody into a roar of excitement while they dance like wild animals.

My mind's foggy as I watch them in the distance. I place my palm to my forehead.

"Let's talk about our future," Spike insists.

I blink, trying to focus on him. "Did you drug us?"

"The herb that ferments in the wine allows you to relax and enjoy the festivities."

"You should have warned me."

"I *should* have?"

I flinch at his tone. "I don't like this feeling. I want to go back to the city." I maneuver around all the bodies and towards the vans, my legs shaking and my thoughts still clouded.

"Come here and sit." Spike helps me lower onto a plastic chair under a large oak tree, away from the fire. I shiver as a wind blows and cools my flushed skin. "Since that night I met you on the streets, I knew you were special. You have strength, power, and beauty."

I cringe as he runs a palm over my cheek. "Uh, thanks. I appreciate your help."

"Good, then you can return the favor by pledging an oath to our pack and becoming my mate. Together we will create the next generation of warriors and run Carson City, side by side."

"That drug must have made you lose your mind. Maybe we should talk again when we're both sober."

"I have never felt more clear-headed. I rescued you that night and molded you for this very moment."

"But I never agreed to this. Why do *you* get to make these choices for me? It's *my* life!" I stand faster than my sedated senses can process, and my vision blurs. I need to get out of here before he does something stupid. But I'm so very tired.

"You're acting like an ungrateful bitch. Sit back down. This isn't up for debate. I will have you as my mate, and you'll learn to respect me. Or you'll be leashed and muzzled for the rest of your pitiful existence." His face contorts as he spits the predictions at me. He is at his breaking point, and if I don't get away from him, his words are not going to be just threats in the wind.

I pray to anyone listening to give me an opportunity—*any* opportunity—to run as far as I can until the liquor has run its course. At that same moment, a gang member screams from across the field as his shirt tail flutters into the flame and catches fire. The poor man wails and waves his drunk arms around like a rotisserie chicken.

My mouth falls open and I rub my lids. Am I seeing things?

Spike curses, chasing after the human torch while pulling his own shirt off in the process. Once he is no longer within reach, I move as fast and far as my legs can carry me. The woods are thick, and I trip often, my skin marred with scrapes and bruises as my lungs protest the exertion. But if I stop now, Spike will kill me. And if I'm gone, who will be left to save Sara?

My world continuously sways as my senses succumb to the drug.

I'm not sure where I'm going, but I hope it's to safety. Suddenly, a thick stump takes me down and I fly into a stream. I gasp as the shock of the cold punches the oxygen from my lungs. I claw my way out of the rushing water and flop onto my back. The starry night sky rotates, resembling a kaleidoscope, before my vision glazes over and darkens at the corners.

Scarlett

Cave Home

"I'm telling you... I found her right outside by the stream."

"You aren't supposed to bring in stray humans, Aspen. You don't know where they've been."

"What was I supposed to do, Sky? Leave her there to die! She was freezing, and nobody was around to help her."

The new voices cause me to stir, but my body protests.

"Oh, she's waking up. Wait, where are you going? Shouldn't she see another female when she comes to? She might be frightened."

"You look female enough, little brother."

I hear a door close before footsteps approach.

"Miss? You are safe. I rescued you from a stream, not too far from our residence."

My eyes flutter open, and I stare into the young man's face. "Where am I?" I croak out.

"You're at my house. I live here with my pack family. Here, take this cup of water. Can you tell me your name and where you're from?"

I lean against the wooden headboard before I blink and take in my surroundings. The walls in the small room resemble stone. "Is this a cave?"

"Yes, it is. My family has lived here for centuries; our ancestors carved out these caves and made them into habitable dwellings." The pride in his voice makes me smile. He is nothing like Spike or the other gang members. He is clean, and his green eyes sparkle with kindness.

Oh no, I forgot about Spike! I jump out of bed, throwing off the covers. "I need to get back."

"Back to where, exactly? You can hardly stand on your own." He helps me lean against the bed. "Please tell me what happened, and maybe I can assist you."

I brush past him to grab the doorknob. I can't endanger him… or his family.

But then he places a hand on my arm. "There's no need to be afraid. We can protect you, no matter what kind of trouble you're in. My name is Aspen."

I wish I could believe his promises, but I shake my head. How many men do I have to watch fall to Spike's wrath? "I appreciate the sentiment, but I'm a loner. I'll just be on my way."

He places his other hand flat on the door, stopping me from opening it. "Let me fetch my mom. She can look you over, then take you wherever you need to go."

"I told you I can find my own way."

"At least have something to eat before you leave."

I let out a breath, knowing this is a battle lost. *For now.* "That sounds great. Thank you, Aspen. My name is Scarlett."

"Scarlett is a beautiful name; it matches your hair color."

I self-consciously run a finger through my dirty locks. "Thanks."

"Why don't you relax in here while I heat up some stew."

"Why can't I go with you?"

"Well, because I haven't told my parents that I brought home a hum—*person*. And they can be protective and bossy, especially if my brother finds out." He smirks. "Do you have any siblings?"

"No, I don't."

"Oh, so you're an only child? That's rare to find these days. It must be quiet at your house."

"Yeah, I guess it is."

"I'll return as quickly as I can. Feel free to watch TV or whatever. I shouldn't be long."

I wait until the door closes, then I collect what I can before moving to the window in the far corner. I slide my hand over it and grin. This house is amazing. The walls are cold like a cave, but it has running water and electricity.

I push at the hinged panels, climb over the ledge, and leap to the ground. When I land, I peek around the corner, in hopes of figuring out which way to go. I lift my nose in the air and attempt to smell something familiar.

There! The faint scent of firewood and oak. That should be the ancestral field. I can only pray there's a town on the way or a little further past.

Sticking to the shadows, I head in that direction, with the last of the sun's rays warming me. When I am far enough from Aspen's cave, I start jogging. Once my muscles warm, I pick up a brisk pace. It feels so freeing to be running for fun, and *not* because somebody's chasing me with a gun. I glance over my shoulder to make sure I'm not *imagining* this unusual situation. But the woods are unquestionably quiet, except for chirping birds and scurrying squirrels.

Soon, my energy depletes and my empty stomach churns. I curse myself for not taking up that offer of food before making my hasty escape. I chew my lip as I slow to a walk while scanning the forest. Because I live in the city, I don't know much about wild berries or herbs. The only education I've received on cooking was from an orphanage volunteer. She loved to watch culinary shows during her breaks. I'd glance over her shoulder and take mental notes.

Maybe I can find something edible out here? Unfortunately, the vegetation looks unfamiliar, and I grumble again, lamenting over my poor planning. I tilt my head skyward and grumble as the sun is almost hidden behind the horizon. In the corner of my eye, I spot a small cave and decide to bunk there for the night. I mean, it can't be any worse than the Warehouse, right? I hone in on the skills I learned on the streets and gather dry moss, sticks, and a few rocks. Then I set them down in the damp cave.

I squeal and fling my arms around like a lunatic, as I unknowingly walk face-first into an enormous spiderweb. Once I triple-check that there are no Black Widows on me, I take in the stone walls. It isn't huge, but it's enough to protect me from the elements and any hungry predators.

I hit the rocks together until they spark a small fire. Then I blow gently, urging the sticks and moss to catch. Once the makeshift blaze is steadily glowing, I lean back and yawn. All this fresh air is going to help me sleep like a baby.

But after an hour, the weather takes a turn for the worst. The wind howls and the icy air forces its way into my sanctuary, making my teeth chatter. I rub my arms and hover over the dwindling flames. "Stay awake or you won't have to worry about Spike killing you, because you'll be a human popsicle."

When my breath comes out in visible puffs, I know the temperatures are dropping fast. I huddle closer to the fire, in a tight ball, and shove my fingers into my armpits.

"In trying to protect others, you've damned yourself. You had to be an idiot and turn down a warm bed, food, *and* a ride home." I shiver uncontrollably, wishing I had gathered more logs for kindling.

My head shoots to the entrance of the cave as I hear something approach—something large. With adrenaline fueling my movements, I sit up and grasp my knife. I lean against the cold wall and pray that *whatever it is* turns away on its own. But the crunching leaves tell me otherwise.

I glance at the fire and wonder if the heat is bringing the intruder closer. I kick at the sparking wood with my boot, and it extinguishes in a poof of smoke. The footsteps cease and I hold my breath. My heart hammers so loudly in my ears I can make out little else. Why can't I catch a break?

"Just come inside and eat me. I'm already half-dead anyway," I chatter to the ominous shadow lurking at the threshold.

The crunching inches closer, and soon I'm staring into the dark pupils of a massive beast. The eyes pierce mine as its ears pin back against its head.

"Shit!" I blurt out. My body fails me and starts convulsing, demanding warmth. Involuntarily, I slide to the floor and curl into a ball, trying to stop the seizure-like motions. So, *this* is how the great Scarlett meets her maker. By freezing to death, before being served up as dinner to a man-eating wolf.

As darkness encompasses my mind, I can't help but laugh at the irony of Spike calling me Little Wolf and my *end* culminating at the foot of one.

Sable

Unnecessary Tool

"**C**huck, grab me the air filter for the Mazda."

"Sure thing, boss."

"Sable, you have company."

I grind my teeth as I attempt to remove a stubborn lug nut. My hand slips and I bust my knuckles. "Fucking piece of shit!" I toss the breaker bar across the bay before shaking out my bleeding hand. I straighten, glare at the car, and kick a tire for good measure. "This better be important, Aspen."

From the doorway that leads to the waiting area, Aspen wiggles his eyebrows. I slam my shoulder into his, not in the mood for his antics. The only reason he's even assisting in the office is because my mother begged me to get him out of the cave for a few hours. Aspen mostly does online classes and is voluntarily den-ridden for days. And she thinks if he's here, he can socialize while spending quality time with me.

"Ouch." He rubs his shoulder. "You know, if you wore the

mechanic gloves I bought you for Christmas that wouldn't have happened."

"I told you they make my grip feel... *off*."

"At least it would save you from embarrassing yourself in front of the ladies when you throw a tantrum."

"I actually like my men rough around the edges." We turn to see a blonde in leather pants and high heels. She extends a polished hand. "We met many moons ago. My name is Bridgett. I'm from Robert's pack."

I accept her palm with mine. "It's nice to see you again."

She takes in my coveralls with a grin. "Your mom said you were interested in a lunch date?"

"Actually, I told her I didn't have time for a date. Just a quick meeting. I'm backed up here and my lunch break isn't for another hour."

She licks her lips as she zeros in on my mouth. "Well, I'm always up for a quickie."

"Chuck and I can watch the shop while you grab a bite," Aspen offers.

I attempt to protest, but Bridgett swiftly wraps an arm around mine and guides me towards the exit. "Thanks, Aspen. You're such a sweetheart."

I shoot my brother a scowl before the door closes behind us. That little shit is getting it when I return. I don't have time for this bullshit. All the bays are full, and two customers are sitting in the waiting area. Ugh... I picked the wrong profession. I should have just taken my degree and worked in a top-notch engineering company. But our little town lacked an automotive shop. And a temporary situation turned into a thriving business. Plus, it keeps me so busy I can easily get out of forced dates and mandatory pack meetings—which means I don't have to be surrounded by the haunting memories of my lost mate. Win-win.

"Do you want to go to my place or yours?"

"Huh?" I blink at her expectant tone. "Neither. Why can't we just do it here."

Her eyes grow wide as she surveys the parking lot. *"Here?"*

"Wait a minute. Are you sure we're talking about the same thing?"

"I thought you wanted to have sex." Her blunt response causes me to cringe.

I scan the area to make sure none of my customers are within earshot. "We don't need to have sex to see if we're mates."

Her curvy body leans into mine, and I almost reconsider my quick dismissal. She runs a fingertip over my chest. "I know we don't *need* to, but it *would be* more fun."

I swallow, as I take in every inch of her tantalizing figure, but ultimately shake my head. "Listen, I appreciate the offer, but I'm only doing this to find my mate."

"Aw, well, that's a shame."

"It's safer this way."

"Safe is boring." She pouts. Then, when she realizes I'm not going to budge, she sighs. "Fine. Let's get it over with then."

Her attitude is grating on my last nerve, so I quickly snatch her chin and dip my lips to hers. Although it feels good, it's definitely not *come in your pants* worthy. Just as I'm pulling away, she wraps her legs around me while shoving her tongue into my throat. I back step and lose my balance. I clutch the nearest thing to steady myself, which happens to be her ass. She takes this as a cue to continue and grinds her core on my crotch. This is not how I want my customers to see me. Or my employees, for that matter.

I take her hips and firmly set her on the ground. Her pout reminds me of my sister's, and I doubt many people have told her no either. "I appreciate your enthusiasm, but I don't think we're mates. I'm sorry you wasted your time driving here."

She narrows her eyes before she pivots and sways her hips to her car. I take a minute to appreciate her assets, then I return to the shop.

"Not a word," I grind out to my brother and employee as they grin at me. "And get back to your stations."

My days pass quickly and by midweek, I am dirty, hungry, and ready to fall flat on my face—all at once.

"Sable! Sable! I need your help!"

"After the stunt you pulled at the shop, I'm not lifting a damn finger for you."

"But—"

I hold up a hand. "It's been one hell of a day, and it's late. So, unless it's a life-or-death situation, ask me again tomorrow." I brush past my brother and stride towards my room, that is, until I catch a whiff of a new scent and freeze. I pivot back towards Aspen. "Who's here?"

"Well, that's the thing I was trying to tell you…"

I growl at him, the strange smell awakening my wolf. "*What* were you trying to tell me?"

"There was this human. I found her in the stream, freezing to death, so I brought her home."

I twist and push open the guest room door. Looking from side to side, I'm disappointed when I don't see her. Aspen taps my shoulder, then points to the open window. I shove my head into the night air and groan. Then I pull back and glare at him. "You lost her? How the hell did you do that?"

"I just left to get her some food. She was starving, Sable. All skin and bones. And when I came back, she was gone. But I had class, and by the time it was over, you were here."

"Does she know we are shifters?"

"No."

I arch a brow at his tone. "Well, I almost slipped a few times, but I'm pretty sure she doesn't know."

I run my hands over my face. "And now she is running around in the woods, at night, in the freezing cold, without any fur."

"That's why I was trying to get your help! Let's go find her!"

"No."

"What? She could die out there."

"I meant: no, as in, you stay here. I'm going after her."

"But…"

"No *buts*. My tracking skills far surpass yours. You stay here in case she returns.""

"Sable," he whines.

I shed my clothes and leap forward, shifting into my fur coat midair.

This is bullshit. I can't believe he brought somebody to the cave. He has no common sense. He should have called emergency services or taken her to the hospital. Instead, I'm stuck cleaning up his mess.

I gallop through the trees, pausing every so often to examine the leaves for her scent. Eventually, I end up at a small clearing. Her smell is strong, but I don't see anybody. Where did she go?

I stomp around the area, grumbling out of both annoyance and exhaustion, until I see a flicker of light. I approach with caution. The flicker goes out in a puff and debris shoots up my nostrils. I cough and growl at the sting.

Son of a bitch! Is she attacking me with dirt?

I hear her trembling, so I close my mouth to hide my fangs. It's only when our eyes meet that I realize her movements aren't due to fear—she is shivering. As I step closer, I take in her appearance. Aspen was right. She isn't healthy and probably hasn't eaten a full meal in a long time.

I tilt my head. Those eyes, and the way she speaks with such ferocity... The combination kindles a spark in my chest that I haven't felt in a while. But I don't have much time to dwell on it, as she collapses to the cold ground. I leap into action and envelop her in the warmth of my coat.

Then, I weigh my options. If I shift back, I can carry her out. But that would likely scare the shit out of her. And who knows if her malnourished heart could sustain the shock. Besides, it'd take a lot of explaining on my part, and I'm dead-ass tired and in no mood for conversation.

My jaw opens wide in a yawn, as I shuffle her crimson locks aside with the tip of my muzzle. Her pulse is steady. Her breathing is rhythmic. I yelp as she turns, wraps her arm around my neck, and tugs. I wheeze against the unintentional choke hold, before she loosens her grip.

Well, I guess I'm camping out here for the night. And tomorrow (*after* I get her something to eat) I'll make sure she returns home.

Scarlett

Wolfie

Why do I smell wet dog? Is this really what heaven smells like?

I gag. *Nope, this has to be hell.* I scrunch my nose as hair tickles my upper lip. I swat the fur away before wiggling back into its warmth. It takes a minute for me to remember my predicament. My eyes pop open, and I scream, leaping up with my knife at the ready.

"What? How?" I sputter the words at the massive white wolf sleeping on the cave floor. My commotion causes the beast to stir, stretching its long front paws while opening its mouth wide to show off huge canines. Then, with sleep still in its eyes, it glares at my knife. "Hey, don't look at me like that. I thought you were trying to eat me for dinner last night."

The wolf stands, shakes the dirt from its pristine coat, and brushes past me. I watch as it lifts its leg and urinates on a nearby tree.

"How charming. Of course, you're a male," I grumble as I stalk out into the early morning sun. I squint at the ball of light. "Why did you abandon me last night?"

I tilt my head towards a familiar sound—there's water flowing close by. I stumble over a bundle of roots but soon find my way to the same stream that had nearly taken me under.

"Yes! Finally, some good news!"

I lift my nose into the air but frown when I can't pick up the smokey scent from the bonfire. Well, now what? I flop into the leaves and kick at an offensive stump. Movement catches my eye, and I pivot towards the wolf as it sits casually by my side, his dark eyes scanning the horizon while his ears twitch when a bird flies overhead.

I arch a brow as I cautiously poke his shoulder. He turns my way with a squint. "I thought I was dreaming last night when you came inside the cave. Did you stay to keep me warm?"

He blinks once, then ignores me to watch the rising sun.

"Well, for your information, I didn't need your help."

He side-glances me, and I swear he rolls his eyes.

I turn my attention to the sun as golden rays reach for the cloudless sky. How long has it been since I've really witnessed a sunrise this beautiful? It's so quiet and peaceful out here. My vision blurs and I swipe at my lashes. "Listen, mutt, I wasn't trying to die, you know? I just was in a hurry to get back before he could hurt Sara. I mean, she should be safe at the orphanage, but what if she escapes and ends up at the Warehouse again?"

The wolf turns to me and angles his head, his iridescent green eyes searching mine.

"I know. I know. It was dumb. Heck! Talking to a dumb dog is just as dumb."

Images of Sara filter through my mind, and I can't stop the stream of tears dripping from my chin. What is going to happen to her? To me?

There's a soft whine before I feel warmth on my lap. When I open my eyes, I see the wolf's paw on my leg. I sniffle. It feels good to talk and get everything off my chest. "Spike wants me to be his wife, but I told him I am only eighteen. I can't be anybody's wife. I can't even take care of myself."

A low growl emits from the beast's throat.

"Yes, you should hate Spike. He is an evil man." I bring my knees to my chest, remembering the blood splattered across his shirt after he killed Stan. "And he wants me to marry him. I know what you're thinking. But I can't say no. If I do, he won't hesitate to kill everything I love and then turn that same blade on me."

The wolf barks, almost as if responding to my plight.

"If I could just save Sara from his anger, I would gladly let him sink his dagger into my chest. I'm a nobody. Not even my parents came looking for me after I was brought to the orphanage."

The wolf stalks to the stream, his eyes reflecting the movement and glimmer of the water. Then he quickly jabs his fangs into a large fish as it swims past, before tossing it my way.

I yelp as the dying creature flops in front of me, blood spurting from the puncture marks embedded in its scales. "Wolfie! Yuck!" The name just spews out, but I like it. It suits him.

Another fish follows the first, and this one nearly hits me. I send a glare in my furry friend's direction, but he ignores the gesture as he pads back to the cave.

"What am I supposed to do with these?" I glance down at the dead fish and smirk. "Oh, I can cook them! Smart boy." I ruffle his head as I drop the fish on the floor of the cave and begin cleaning them. After a few impatient minutes, he nuzzles my elbow, his tongue protruding as he tastes the air. "Ew. Keep that drool inside your mouth. I need to clean these, so we don't choke on their bones. Then I need to start a fire to cook them."

He stalks out and returns with a pile of sticks in his mouth. I scratch behind his ears and ignite the kindling. I do my best to recall how the chef on the cooking show made their restaurant-quality dish. Although the final result won't win me any awards, it's better than nothing.

"Is it okay if I call you Wolfie?" He yawns, and I take it as a sign of agreement. "Great." I massage my neck. "Listen, what I said earlier, don't go and tell your wolf friends, okay? It's only between us."

He rubs his head on my shoulder, and I scratch his belly. I'm enjoying his companionship, but as they say: all good things must come to an end. Eventually.

"I appreciate the listening ear and breakfast. But I need to be on my way before it gets too late." I stretch out and step away from him, but he whimpers and tugs at my shirt with his teeth. "You know what? You should come with me and eat Spike… and solve all my problems."

He releases his grip and looks out into the distance. I follow his line of sight and can only imagine what he is thinking. Does he really want to kill Spike? Or is it something else?

"You'd miss your family too much." I pet his scruff, already feeling the loss of our impromptu friendship. "I wish I had a family that would miss me. I mean a real family. One who'd love me and not expect anything in return." I brush past him with a heavy heart.

Once I'm walking along the stream again, I straighten my spine and chastise myself. "Enough playing around. It's time to return to reality."

I take in a deep breath and force one foot in front of the other. Then I sneak a peek over my shoulder, and sure enough, Wolfie is sitting where I left him—he's watching me.

"Goodbye," I whisper, in an attempt to ignore the ache in my chest.

Sable

Trap

Seeing Scarlett fade into the distance was the hardest thing I've ever done. That is, until she pivots at the last minute and mouths a farewell with shimmering eyes. And it feels like my heart is being torn open, thrown on the ground, and stomped to shit.

After everything she just confided in me, my wolf begs to extend his fierce protection, to be her *fur hero*. Hell, he even accepted the nickname Wolfie—which she seemed to coin sporadically. Although it is unoriginal and has a girlie feel to it, he doesn't mind as long as *she* is setting aside a unique title just for *him*.

I wince as her shadow melts into the tree line. But I have other matters to attend to first… before I unleash the beast and fight for her freedom from the Fangs.

A growl rips through my throat at the name. Yes, I am very familiar with their reign of terror in Carson City. And more specifically, with their leader: Spike Fangs. That hairy dictator comes from a long line of rebels and merciless alphas. They have no limit when it comes to their schemes, bending and twisting Luna's laws in order to justify their actions.

At any cost, even innocent lives.

I snort at the thought of Spike's brother, Mark. After they lost their parents, they lived peacefully among the Tala pack—up until Mark came of age and decided to challenge their alpha, Frost. Mark lost the fight and retreated with his tail between his legs. Then, when Frost had his back turned, Mark jumped him from behind, in hopes of ripping open his throat. Instead, the fool forced his opponent's hand *and* caused unnecessary bloodshed. Mark's wounds were severe, and he bled out at Spike's feet. Unable to find humility even with his last breath, Mark continued his ancestors' mistakes, spewing threats of revenge and further violence.

Although Frost was victorious, he still bares the scar and haunting memories of that day. And he never got over the regret of killing Mark and orphaning Spike, so he allows Spike to rule Carson City with his little pack of misfits. Even though we always knew they were keeping company with humans, I never expected him to want to marry one.

That is unheard of.

Besides the obvious fact that Luna designates a mate for every wolf, and that mate is *not* a human, we can't produce the next generation of shifters if we were to comingle. We can bear children together, but fur will never spring from their skin.

So, the question remains on the tip of my tongue: what the fuck is Spike up to?

Obviously, he is using this Sara girl to manipulate Scarlett, but what are his actual motives? Why waste energy on a human if he wants to continue his bloodline of wolves? Don't get me wrong, Scarlett is far from an ordinary human. She's fierce, strong, and her scent did something weird to my wolf that I can't put a paw on. Did Spike get the same vibes? Is that why she is important to him?

Either way, I need to warn my parents about the situation. Maybe they could help keep Scarlett and Sara safe. Or, at the very least, they can consult with Frost and build a plan of action. Because no human (or shifter) should be manipulated like Scarlett has been. Spike has gone too far.

Not to mention, he brought her to the sacred grounds! That ancestral land is for shifters and our Native American protectors only. Bringing an outsider is against the rules and basically spitting on your descendants. I cringe at the thought. I wonder… Did he have her and the other humans drink the ceremonial wine too...? The same liquid that represents an unspoken oath to commit yourself to the pack.

With a newfound urgency, I gallop towards my family's cave as fast as my four legs can carry me, leaping over fallen logs and avoiding new saplings. But with each thunderous step, my wolf hesitates. He doesn't want to move farther away from Scarlett, and he is fighting me at every turn, no matter how much I remind him the distance is only *temporary*. That once the alphas are alerted, we will sneak behind enemy lines, steal her, and whisk her away. *To a life she deserves.*

Suddenly, a searing pain rips up my back leg and I collapse. Fire burns throughout my body and I howl in agony. I attempt to shift, but whatever inferno has set my wound ablaze is also coursing through my veins and hindering my abilities.

Scarlett

New Friends

I focus on the birds fluttering overhead, the rabbits scurrying in search of potential clovers hidden amongst the dead vegetation. Anything, *but* the fact that my feet feel like lead the farther I drag them away from Wolfie.

Eventually, my mind wanders to what Spike said about marriage. I never thought I would survive long enough to even consider the possibility in my future. I had one job in life: make it to tomorrow.

My lips twitch at the thought of having somebody to love… to be *loved*. My eyes drop to my black tactical pants and faded grey button-up shirt. My choice in apparel isn't exactly feminine… Come to think of it, I don't own a dress or even heels. And isn't that what men want in a wife? Attractiveness, class, and manners?

Yeah, well, I have none of that.

Does Spike really want to love and protect me, or is this only a convenience for him? What did he say in his impromptu proposal?

That I had strength, power, and beauty. I bite my lip as his face comes to mind. Maybe with the drug out of his system, he's returned to his senses and realizes how stupid marrying me would be.

My head shoots up as I hear an earth-shattering howl. Then my heart bursts to life as I take off towards the sound while chanting, "Please don't let that be who I think it is."

I skid around a corner of overgrowth, and there he is: Wolfie, with a bear trap clamped on his hind leg.

"What the hell happened? I thought you were smarter than this."

He growls, baring his teeth.

"I can help, but you need to remain calm, because I sure as hell am not getting bit today. So cool it, or you can just lie here until whoever set this trap comes back to collect your hide."

He rests his head in the grass and squeezes his eyes shut, soft whimpers escaping his clenched jaw.

"Okay, let me see what we have here. It looks like I need to push on these springs, but you'll have to pull your leg free as soon as you can, so it doesn't clamp back down." I place my hands on the cold steel and cringe as blood oozes. With as much force as I can muster, I bear down on the springs to compress them; the coils lower and relieve pressure on the teeth. "Move your leg now."

He winces but pulls his limb free. Then I release the pressure and step back as it snaps shut with a resounding clang. I swipe at my forehead as Wolfie licks his pride. Unbuttoning my shirt, I approach him like the wild animal he is. His head shoots up and he growls.

"Hold still and let me bandage your cut so you aren't bleeding everywhere. The last thing you need is a predator to follow your tracks and eat you for an afternoon snack." I tie it quickly—before he can snap at me—scan the woods, and groan. Wolfie needs somebody more skilled to look after him. And he most definitely can't take care of himself. "Where is your pack? Will they come and help you, boy?"

I kneel in the dirt to run my fingertips through his soft fuzz. He rubs his head on my hand before he licks it. I stare into his eyes and see pain etched in their depths. He needs medical attention.

Spike will have to wait a little longer for my return. I owe Wolfie my life. "I know somewhere I can bring you, so you can get checked out, but you need to walk or let me carry you. Either way, it's going to suck."

Wolfie stands and hobbles in the direction of Aspen's home. I stride beside him, to keep warm and offer him my help.

"It is just a little further," I coax as he slows to a crawl. "It's only right up this hill and around the bend."

Wolfie slumps to the ground. Then he raises his muzzle to the sky and howls deeply.

I lift his massive frame. "Dude, you seriously need to lose weight. Maybe this injury is a good start for you." I put one foot in front of the other, shifting his oversized body and grumbling as sweat drips into my eye.

When the familiar cave house comes into view, my heart fills with joy. On my approach, the inhabitants, which include Aspen and who I can only assume are his family members, race forward. "What happened to him, Scarlett? Are you hurt too?" Aspen looks me over.

"No, I'm fine. I found him caught in a bear trap. He is bleeding and weak. Please tell me you can help him?" Fresh tears sting my eyes as exhaustion replaces the adrenaline fueling my body. And once Wolfie's weight is lifted from my shoulders, I slump while inhaling deeply.

I follow as the family rushes him to a bedroom. There, they clean his wound, check for muscle damage, and apply antibacterial cream. Soon, he is fast asleep on top of a soft comforter in a large king-size bed.

"Scarlett these are my parents: Phoenix and Celeste Canis."

I offer a hand to the two tall figures. "I'm sorry I bothered your family. I didn't know where else to take him."

"You did a heroic deed. No need to apologize. You look exhausted, my dear." Celeste nods towards the other female. "Sky, please grab our guest some clothes and a fresh towel." Then she turns her soft gaze to me. "Please shower and rest. We will have food available soon."

After they leave and the room is quiet, I settle by the fur ball and stroke his ear. Then I nuzzle my face into his neck. "You big idiot. Don't go stepping into anymore traps. Do you hear me?"

He nudges me with his wet nose before licking my tears. I giggle and hold him as tight as I can.

"Don't get any ideas, mutt. I'm leaving at first light… and going back to Spike."

A deep growl rumbles in his chest, and I step back, blinking at his response. But before I can react, Sky returns with her hands full.

"Thank you for the clothes. I'm guessing they are yours?"

"Yes, they're mine, but it's the least I can do, considering you saved Sable."

I arch a brow and glance back at the animal. "His name is Sable?" I taste the word. "Does he come around here often?"

Sky laughs but stops when the wolf barks. "Yes, he practically lives here." She pivots on her heels and strides out before I can question her further.

"Sable, huh? That doesn't seem very fitting for a wild beast. I think I will just stick to Wolfie." I ruffle his fur, but he winces. "Do you want me to call you Sable?" I grumble and rub my palm over my face. "Why am I asking you?"

He crawls closer to me, licking my hand and wagging his tail.

"Pfft, you are fine. I should turn down their hospitality and return home tonight. I wonder if Aspen is still willing to give me a ride into town?"

Sable clamps down on my shirt with his teeth as I walk towards the door. Then I'm yanked onto the bed with him.

"Easy! I don't own a lot of clothes." I finger a hole near the seam and glare at him. "That's two shirts you owe me, fart breath." Then I eye the bloody shirt in the hamper by the door—the one recently removed from his leg. "And *that one* was my favorite. Heck, it was my warmest."

I glide my palm over the soft sweater Sky handed me. This small act of kindness is the nicest thing anybody has ever done for me. I make a note to thank her again. A cold nose nudges me towards the bathroom.

"Fine, I get the hint."

Sable

Furever

*O*nce the bathroom door closes, I lean in to the pillow, exhausted as I fight the pain shooting up my leg. I can't believe I didn't see that trap! Good thing Scarlett heard my call before whoever set it found me. And now, for some reason, I can't change forms. This shitshow keeps getting better and better...

"Sable?" My head shoots up and my ears pivot. My mom closes my door softly prior to transforming into a snow-white wolf. She pads over, wincing through her teeth as she licks my muzzle and buries her face in my neck.

I return the welcome. Then, meeting her gaze, I listen as her words are conveyed through our connection. *"That poor girl, she is all skin and bones. Where did you find her?"*

"It's a long story. You should ask Aspen to explain it. Why can't I shift?"

She tilts her head and glances towards my wound. *"I'm not sure. I'm sending Aspen to dispose of the trap and explore the surrounding* area. *My biggest concern is making sure there are no more and to discover who set them out.*"

"*I would bet my money on Spike.*"

"*Spike? But his territory is in Carson City? Why would he be lurking in ours?*"

"*I believe he is searching for Scarlett.*"

"*Why?*" I explain everything I've learned during my time with Scarlett—all of which sends my mom's wolf growling. She has always had a soft spot for children. And learning that Spike is threatening one does not sit well. *"That bastard! I'll rip him apart!"*

"*I have a more productive idea. Is Debbie still looking for a little girl to adopt?*"

Mom tilts her head. "*That's a great idea! I will give her a call. And maybe we can help both girls find new homes? Then Spike won't be able to harass them.*"

"*Should we explain everything to Frost?*"

"*No, I'm sure he has enough to worry about with his own pack, especially with preparing the pups for their first hunt. I'll tell him when it's necessary, but for now, we'll do our best to take care of it.*"

Not being able to shift sucks. I don't know how I'm supposed to make it into work tomorrow, because I sure as hell can't hold my tools. Unless... maybe I can fit them in my mouth?

"*Rest,*" my mom commands. "*I'll call the shop and tell them you are ill and can't come in for a few days. That way, it'll buy us some time to sort everything out.*"

Shit! What if I'm never able to switch back, and I'm trapped in this fur suit forever?

Scarlett

Drawing Battle
Lines

I close the door and glance around the ceramic palace. There is an enclosed walk-in shower, a wide jacuzzi tub, two dazzling sinks, and a separate closet area with a toilet. How can they afford all of this? Who *are* these people?

Once I get past my shock, I start the shower. What the heck? The sprayer has ten different options, including LED lights. I finally figure out the right settings and relax under the steady stream. As I glance down, I can't help but notice the swirls of blood retreating into the drain. Between the sudden change in temperature and my hypnotic trance, I find myself lightheaded, so I lean my forehead on the stone while visions of Sable lying on the ground pass through my mind.

I've never owned a pet before. The closest I've come was at the orphanage when I would speak to the roaches before they scurried under my bed. And I'm guessing that doesn't count. But with Wolfie, I mean *Sable,* it feels different—special even. His attentiveness shows that he really cares about what I'm saying, whether he understands it or not. And that feels so good, especially after being invisible all these years. Maybe I can adopt him and bring him back to the city with me?

I snort as I shut off the faucet and get dressed. The city is no place for a dog, let alone one as obviously spoiled as the beast in the king-size bed. Plus, how would I care for him? I have no job, nor a place to stay. And Spike wouldn't even consider letting a mutt into the Warehouse.

Once I change and enter the bedroom, I stroke Sable's soft fur and watch his chest steadily rise and fall. And a sort of peace rests in my heart. No. He'd never be happy with me, and he deserves so much more than what I have to offer.

"Hey, Scarlett. Mom asked me to tell you that dinner is ready."

"Thank you." I bite my trembling lip. "Aspen, it's going to be difficult… saying goodbye to him tomorrow."

"Well, tomorrow is so far away. Why don't we just stay in the present and *enjoy* what we have right now? Like new friendships." He wraps an arm around my neck and guides me to the kitchen. Then we sit at the table while Celeste serves beef stew with dinner rolls.

"Thank you, Celeste. Everything looks wonderful."

"It is the least I could do for our hero."

My face heats. "I've been called many colorful things, but nobody has ever called me anything close to *that* before."

"Maybe they just don't know you as well as they should. I mean, how many people do you know who would risk their life to bring an injured animal to safety?"

"Well, Sable saved my life first. I owed him."

"You didn't *owe* him, dear. You had compassion for him. Just like you have compassion for others too. Am I right?"

I pause mid-bite but shrug off her question. She has no idea who I am. Just because I helped an animal, it doesn't mean I'm a good person. What would they say if they knew what I've done for a hot meal and a warm bed? I'm far from perfect.

"Mom, I found where that trap's located. It's just past the stream, two paces over our border. And you were right; there was a sticky film on the blades. I left a sample of it in your office."

"Thank you, dear. I'll run some tests and see what we're dealing with. But at least we know why the wound caused this much damage and he couldn't..." Her eyes dart to mine. "He couldn't walk."

"Who do you think set them?" I frown at Celeste.

But it's Sky who answers. "A group of people were at the meadow a few nights ago. They probably got rowdy and left some parting gifts."

"That seems like a little bit of a stretch. I mean, if they came and went, why would they leave a trap."

"Because they are inconsiderate pricks. Every year, they visit, have their little powwow, and try to start trouble with the locals on their way out," Sky spits.

Aspen pats my hand. "They're part of a gang known for their brutality. But don't worry, they all went back home. We just need to double-check the property lines for any other surprises they may have left behind."

71

I push my plate aside, unable to eat another bite as my stomach churns. Had Spike been *that* close to Aspen's home? If so, things are far worse than I anticipated. I need to return to Carson City so he can't cause any more damage. But before I can scurry off, Phoenix shuffles a deck of cards. "It's tradition for our family to play a quick game after a meal together. Why don't you join in on the fun? Do you know how to play poker?" He tosses cards around the table without waiting for my reply.

I peek at everyone's smiling faces and hold back a sob, touched by their willingness to include me. "I know my way around the game."

"Perfect! Let's have a quick round before going to bed." The *quick round* turns into two hours of laughing, yelling, and me whooping their asses. And it feels wonderful to be good at something that *doesn't* involve stealing.

During the match, I learn that Phoenix is a professor at the local university, where he teaches anatomy and physiology. Sky owns and manages a steakhouse. Aspen is a freelance writer, with dreams of starting his own publishing company and bookstore. And Celeste works at the hospital on a Native American reservation not too far from here; she mostly does video appointments and small lab tasks, though she does conduct in-person rotations once or twice a week.

"I'm actually stopping by the reservation tomorrow, to drop off a very important package to a dear friend. I can drive you home afterwards, if you want, Scarlett. Where exactly did you say you lived?"

"Currently, I'm living in Carson City."

"Oh. Well. That is an interesting place. Have you been there long?"

"As long as I can remember, yes."

"What do you do for work? Do you enjoy it?"

"Oh, I don't have a job... yet." I leave out the fact that I don't have a permanent address either.

"Well, you are still young, dear. I'm sure you will find the *perfect* job. And if you can't find employment in Carson City, you can always work here in Cold Creek. I know Sky is constantly looking for new servers and kitchen staff at her restaurant. And the hospital is desperate for eager helping hands. I would be honored to give you a letter of recommendation."

"Yes, and the university has a massive list of untapped scholarships. If you prefer to elevate your education, I could *effortlessly* get you enrolled... should that be the route you want to travel." Phoenix beams.

Wait, why are they all so willing to help a worthless homeless person? They are offering to put their necks on the line for *me*. Their generosity causes my lip to quiver, and to save myself the embarrassment, I look down at my folded hands.

"We didn't mean to upset you, dear. You, of course, don't have to work or go to school if you are happy with your current arrangement. We are only doing what we do best, being nose-butting parents."

"You didn't upset me. I'm not used to such kindness, especially from strangers."

"Yeah, because Carson is filled with thugs and murderers," Sky scoffs.

"Skylar," Phoenix warns.

I meet the young woman's eyes. She isn't wrong, but what choice do I have? I clear my tightened throat and push back my chair. "I should go check on the dog." I can't make eye contact with them as I trudge towards the bedroom.

73

"Wait up, Scarlett. I'm sorry if Sky made you feel uncomfortable. She has no filter at times." Aspen rubs his neck.

"It's fine, really. She is absolutely right. Carson City is a mess."

"Then why do you stay there?"

"It's complicated."

"I understand… Well, have a good night." Aspen pivots before shoving his hands in his pockets. I know he wants to help, but I can't risk his family getting hurt.

I snuggle under the covers before draping my arm over Sable's velvety coat—carefully—so I don't wake him. Then I nuzzle into the soft pillows and release a content sigh. Returning to the city is going to be a challenge for sure. I have been thoroughly pampered. As I drift off to sleep, I ponder: *Is this how typical families feel? Safe, warm, and full?* I hum at the thought. After all, a girl could get used to this.

Sable stirs, and I pull him closer. "Don't leave me," I whine.

"Okay, five more minutes." My sleepy brain takes a moment to process that the *dog* is speaking to me. Am I still dreaming? I peek through my lashes, to confirm my current state of consciousness, when I see a man sleeping next to me. A *naked* man sleeping next to me. Hmm… a *very handsome,* naked man sleeping next to me… *WAIT!*

I flop out of bed and scramble to locate my knife. "Who are you!" His eyelids flutter open, and I gasp as the green of Sable's irises stare back at me. "Where the hell is the wolf? What did *you* do with Sable? If you hurt him, I'll kick your ass!"

The man blinks down at his arms. "The poison must have worn off..."

Suddenly, the bedroom door flies open, and Phoenix barges in with a long ninja-looking sword. But once he notices the mystery man, he drops his defensive stance. "Thank Luna you're all right, son."

I watch—still in shock—as the entire family trickles in to check on the man's leg. "What the hell is going on? Have I lost my mind? Wait, no. I *must* be dreaming." I frantically dig my knuckles into my eyes. "How do I wake up!" I slap myself but flinch as my cheek registers the sting.

The room is too quiet. I slowly tilt my head and realize that everybody is staring at me with arched brows. Like *I'm* the crazy one! To further cement their opinions of me, I throw my hands up and run out of the room as fast as I can. Whatever voodoo shit is going on, I want nothing to do with any of it! I yelp when something tugs at my arm.

"Wait. Please let me explain."

Instinctively, I bring the knife to my attacker's throat. "Release me, immediately."

A grin slowly spreads over his face. "You would do that to *me*? Your Wolfie?" The familiar pet name is like a blow to my chest. This guy's whole demeanor... the way he looks at me... it all screams *Sable*, but he's *so* not a wolf. And he's definitely missing a lot of fur. He releases me, and I turn to run again. But his quick reflexes have him blocking my path before I can get much space between us. "We should talk."

"Let me go. I promise I won't tell anyone what I saw." My offer hangs in the air as the man in front of me transforms into the wolf I hold close to my heart. My knife clatters to the floor. I sway and collapse onto my rear. "What the…"

Wolfie, Sable, the guy—whatever he is—licks my face and sits in front of me.

I shake my pounding head and shoo him back. "No. This can't be real."

"Scarlett, dear, I'm sorry we didn't tell you sooner. Sable asked us to wait until he had a chance to explain," Celeste soothes.

"Yeah, because he knew you would freak out like this." Sky rolls her eyes. "I'm late for work. Good luck, brother. You are going to need it." Sable whimpers as he pads to the front door beside her. And I watch as they stride out as if it's an everyday occurrence.

"How about some coffee?" Aspen offers a hand.

"Are you all like *him*?"

He cringes at my harsh tone. "Yes, we are all shifters."

"Shifters?" I try to grasp the meaning of the word. Before I can make up my mind to either run or stay, Sable returns—in human form. I pivot away from his unapologetic nakedness, trying to hide my inevitable blush. He ruffles my hair as he passes with a laugh.

Why am I so turned on by this fur god? Maybe it's the horndog pheromones he's putting out? I bet all women act like this towards him.

"Once you eat something and have time to digest this information, I'm sure you'll feel better." Phoenix leads us into the kitchen.

I must be nuts. Why am I still sitting here, surrounded by a pack of wolves? Oh, that's right, because they could easily catch me if I tried to flee. My leg bounces while I stare at Sable as he lowers himself into the chair across from me. Thank goodness he put on some clothing! He's now wearing jeans and a black t-shirt. Although he is fully covered, my mouth waters remembering the provocative images from earlier. When he meets my gaze, I quickly turn away. I can't believe what I saw. How could a human be an animal and vice versa?

"Do you still want me to bring you home, dear?" Celeste passes me some waffles.

"Are we just going to ignore the huge *elephant* in the room?" I pout.

"You mean the *wolves* in the room?" Aspen elbows with a grin.

I suck in a breath. "You know what? I need a minute away from all of this." I push past the exit.

"Scarlett, come on. We were doing so good in there." Sable saunters up beside me.

I pivot and poke a finger into his chest as he towers over my much smaller frame. "I woke up next to a *naked* man. The same man who just the night before wasn't a man at all. We were *not* doing good."

"Aw, have I offended those virgin eyes of yours?"

"We are not discussing my sex life."

Sable processes my words before he clenches his fists. "You mean, Spike and you… that dirtbag! Did he force himself on you?"

I cringe at his intensity. I forgot how much I'd told him, back when I thought he couldn't understand me. "That is none of your damn business." My voice wavers with the humiliation. "You could never understand what I've had to endure! Because *you've* had everything given to you on a silver platter. A family, a roof over your head, and food on the table. When have you ever had to fight for your survival?" I expect a myriad of responses from him: yelling, reprimanding, throwing shit around.

But what I don't expect is him embracing me, or speaking softly into my ear as he rubs my back. "Hey, I'm sorry. You're right. It *is* none of my fucking business." He rests his chin on my head and breathes in. "I've wanted to hug you ever since you told me you were worthless. Because you aren't. I hope you know that. You deserve so much more than what you have. Or don't have."

The sentiment tugs at my heartstrings. I wrap my arms around him and squeeze my eyes to keep the tears from spilling over. Why is life so cruel? "Stop filling me with hope. It's going to make returning to the city that much more difficult for me."

"Then don't leave; stay here with us. We will protect you."

"I'm just a lousy human. Why would you or your family want to help me? I'm a nobody." I push away from him—and his empty promises—before swiping at my eyes. Once my vision clears, I see his family watching us.

"We didn't mean to intrude on your conversation." Celeste wipes her damp cheeks. "We just wanted to check on you... to make sure you were okay." They really do care for this stupid human. *For me.* Before I can respond, something in the bushes draws my attention. My words catch in my throat as three large shadows approach.

Sable pivots towards the origin of my distress, shoving me behind him. "You are trespassing. Leave now and no harm will come to your pack." Sable's family gathers by his side, narrowing their eyes at the beasts continuing to stalk our way. I can't withhold my gasp as the wolves shift into human form.

Oh no. I backpedal, my fingertips covering my mouth. It's worse than anything I could have imagined... I stumble over a tree root, before landing flat on my butt as the realization sinks in: not only is *he* ruthless but he's also a shifter.

"She doesn't belong to you." Spike's voice roars louder than I've ever heard.

"She doesn't belong to anybody, you twisted bastard." Sable takes a step forward with balled fists.

"I'm not leaving without my property, *boy*. Why am I even speaking to you, beta?" He dismisses Sable and turns to Phoenix. "Alpha to alpha, I demand you hand her over, and then we'll be on our way."

They can't risk their lives for me. I won't allow it. I scramble to my feet and stride towards my living nightmare. When he meets my gaze, his anger burns brighter than ever. And I know there is going to be hell to pay. If he even allows me to live, I'll be pleasantly surprised. Before I can brush past my protectors, Sable grabs my wrist. Our eyes meet, and he shakes his head, turning his attention back to Spike.

Phoenix stands tall as he draws his sword and points the tip at my would-be captor. "If you're looking to harm *any* of us, we will fight back. This is your one and only warning."

"Hah, if you think I can't handle a bunch of inexperienced, pampered pups, you're sadly mistaken." He ignores the shifters and targets me. "Scarlett, are you willing to let innocent people die for your own selfish reasons? You're an ungrateful whore. Just you wait until I get you back home."

Sable transforms, and before the threat even has time to settle, his wolf alter ego is pouncing on Spike. They tumble in the brush until Sable has Spike pinned and his teeth bared. I can only stare, watching in awe, as Sable's family follows suit, shifting and lining up in support of their pack. All around me chests rumble, mouths foam, and tensions are thick.

I bite my fingernails, teetering between helpless and hopeless. "Stop! You don't need to fight over me!" I shout to deaf ears. I pull out my knife, grit my teeth, and take a running leap towards one of Spike's wolves as they clamp down on Aspen's throat. The impact knocks the breath from my lungs, and we roll around until the attacker pins me beneath him. Saliva drips onto my chest, and the canine snaps at my nose. "I don't want to hurt you, but I can't let you hurt my friends either."

His weight shifts as he transforms into a human. "You're always getting yourself into these situations, Scarlett."

I can only blink at the man on top of me. I run a shaky fingertip over his bloodied face, to make sure my eyes aren't playing tricks on me. "Tanner, is that you? What happened to you?" Before he can respond, he's slammed to the ground. I watch as Aspen growls and tries to lock his jaw around his opponent's throat, but Tanner only appears to be defending himself, not counterattacking. "Aspen, stop! He isn't fighting you anymore!"

Aspen's eyes glow; they're wild and unrelenting. Is his wolf too hellbent on revenge?

"Aspen, please!" I wave my hands in front of his face, trying to reach his humanity. "You are not a monster!"

The wolf snaps at my outstretched hand and I back up, cradling my injury. Once the first blood is drawn, Tanner shifts into wolf form, shoving Aspen onto the grass with a loud thump. Having subdued his rival, Tanner reverts to two legs. "Get a grip! I'm done fighting with you." Aspen calms, and Tanner collects me in an embrace. "Spike said they were holding you against your will. Otherwise, I never would have attacked."

Tanner is ripped away, his words still echoing in my head as Spike growls down at him. "Traitor! You had him right where you wanted him, and you let him live!"

Tanner lands a punch to Spike's jaw. "You're a liar. How could you drag us here when she doesn't even want to come back? You put us all in danger under false pretenses! You don't deserve to be alpha." Oh no. I know *that* look... He is beyond seeing red; he's out for blood. And, unfortunately, Tanner is on the path of his destruction.

"Spike, no!" I freeze as a deafening crunch resounds among the woodlands. Spike turns his madness towards me, but Phoenix and Aspen slam into him. I kneel over the motionless figure. "Tanner? Please get up." He moves his hand towards my tear-stained face, but before his fingertips can reach me, he gurgles and his arm falls to the ground. "No. No. No. You have to wake up! Get up!"

I crumble on top of him, begging anyone who is listening to bring my friend back. But I know it's too late. And it's all my fault.

Scarlett

Maya

Everything happens in a blur as police officers surround us and take Spike and the other wolf away in handcuffs.

"This is all your fault, you little shit," Spike spits at me as they pull him away. "None of this would have happened if you'd just stayed where you belong. You could have saved him. His blood is on your hands now." His words burn, and I look away from his contorted rage as he is manhandled to the police car.

"Please don't listen to him. Don't believe that nonsense." Celeste sighs. "He is an angry man, taking his rage out on the wrong person."

"He's right, you know. I could have walked away, and everybody would be fine. What have I done?" My eyes trail over the blood and fur littering the ground. I promised I wouldn't let anybody get hurt. And I've failed.

"Come inside and warm yourself by the fire." Phoenix guides me into the house, where our deserted breakfast still sits.

"Where is Aspen and Sable?"

"The paramedics took them to get checked out. I could have looked them over here, but I didn't want to make a fuss. Let them cool off at the hospital."

"I'm so sorry."

"They knew the risks before they jumped into the fight. We will visit them as soon as we clean up and my package is dropped off." Celeste smiles. "Let me help you with your hand."

I flop onto the couch and watch the flickering fireplace. Crimson catches my eye and I glance at my shirt. It's covered in blood, and at this point, I'm not even sure *whose*. I wince as an alcohol wipe grazes over my bite mark and pulls me out of my despair.

"Well, the good news is we don't need to get you sutured up. Aspen must have been just warning you off."

"Aspen was gone, and the wolf was in control."

"Sweetheart, our wolf is a part of us. We are not two separate entities."

I rub my bandaged hand. "I should get a rabies shot."

She chortles. "My dear Scarlett. You have brought such excitement into my home, thank you." Her kindness engulfs me before sending me over the edge. When she sees my tears, she hugs me and rubs my back. "Let it out, sweetheart." The doorbell chimes and Celeste excuses herself. From the entryway, I hear her say, "Thank you so much for coming. I'll make sure she gets to where she needs to go."

"Thank you again, Dr. Canis. We really appreciate your generous donation and your offer to personally handle this delivery," a man responds.

"It's not a problem. I look forward to seeing the progress on your upgrades to the center." Her voice softens. "Come on in, sweetheart. Don't be scared. We are all friends here. Nobody will hurt you. Do you want something to eat or drink?"

When they turn the corner, I leap out of my chair. "Sara! What are you doing here?"

We embrace, and she wets my shirt with her tears as her tiny body heaves. "I didn't think I would ever see you again," she blubbers out.

"Here are some chocolate chip cookies and milk, Sara." Celeste puts the plate and cup on the table. "I'll let you two catch up while I get the car ready."

I guide Sara to the goodies. "I'll be right back." Then I follow Celeste. "Wait. Why is Sara here? How do you know her?"

"Scarlett, when Sable caught us up on who you were and what happened, we took matters into our own hands. To make sure Sara would be safe. And I know a family on the reservation who has been searching for a young lady to adopt."

"Why would you do that for me? And for her?"

"Compassion shouldn't have limits. Pay it forward one day, okay?" I nod and turn to leave, but she continues, "Could we keep our furry little secret between us, for now? I don't want to overwhelm her."

"Yes, of course." I don't add in that Sara would never believe me, even if I tried to explain the situation to her. Once I make my way back to the kitchen, I settle next to the little girl in question and touch her hand to make sure she is real.

"These cookies are great. Try one."

"I can't handle sugar right now. So much has happened, and my head is spinning."

Sara shoves a cookie between my lips. "Just eat it." I blink before pulling half the cookie out of my mouth. Then we laugh together. It feels good to be with her again… to know she is safe.

"All right, ladies, the car is packed and ready for our trip," Celeste sings as she offers Sara a hand. "Scarlett, I've set some of Sky's clothes on the bed for you, so you can change before we head out."

Sara takes in my disheveled appearance, but I just shrug it off. "I had a nosebleed earlier."

"Thank you again for finding me a home, Dr. Canis."

"Please call me Celeste, Sara. And it's not a problem. After reviewing your file, I know you are a perfect match for my friends."

"I can't wait to meet them."

"They're excited to meet you too, sweetie."

I change and then we get on the road. The drive isn't long, and it sure beats walking. I watch as trees pass in a green blur. What will I do now? If Spike gets out of jail, he'll inevitably come after me. This isn't over.

"We just have to make a quick pit stop to pick up my sons, Sara."

I am pulled out of my misery as we walk into the hospital. "What took you so long? We were ready to leave an hour ago." I hear Sable grumble. When I turn the corner, his eyes lock on mine. "Scarlett, are you okay?" He examines the scratches on my hand, his touch sending warm tingles up my arm.

"I'm fine."

"Listen, what happened back there…"

"You should have let me go with Spike." I glare at him as I brush past.

"What? Why? So he could force you to do his bidding? Fuck that! You will never go back to that sick mutt if I have a say in it."

I narrow my eyes at his overbearing tone. "Well, then it's a good thing you *don't* have a say in it."

Aspen tugs me away from Sable and into a tight hug, knocking the wind out of me. "I'm so sorry. Can you forgive me?"

I rest my head on his shoulder and squeeze. "If you bite me again, I will shove my blade so far up your…"

"He bit you?" We all turn to Sara as she frowns at my bandaged hand, then up at Aspen.

"It was a playful love bite, right, Aspen?" I wink at him before looking back to Sara. My lie works, because Sara wrinkles her nose and shakes her head, muttering "gross" as we walk out. And I know she won't ask again.

Aspen wraps an arm around my neck. "So, it was a love bite, huh?"

"Do you want to test me? Go ahead and try for another one, fleabag."

He grins down at me. "I might have to take that risk."

"You will not. Or you'll have me to answer to." Sable scowls at his brother's draped arm. Aspen quickly removes it before stepping away.

My chuckle is short-lived as we reach the car. The vehicle is small, especially since Celeste insists both of the guys ride in the back seat with me, so that Sara can get the best view of her new town. I'm overheating with their beast-sized bodies pressed up against mine. Out of the corner of my eye, I see Sable resting his head on the window, his lids pinched shut. He must still be in pain.

I lean towards him and whisper, "Why did you tell Celeste about me and Sara?"

"Does it surprise you that an animal *like me* cared and wanted to help?"

"I never said that."

"It was your tone that said it."

"My tone is always like this." He scoffs at my logic and closes his lids again. I *have been* giving off bitchy vibes. And he did put his neck on the line for me. I stare out the windshield and wait until we maneuver around a few bends before swallowing my pride and sharing some gratitude. "Thank you for helping Sara, Sable."

I don't expect an answer back. I just need him to know how I feel. Because as much as I appreciate his recent kindness, his attacking Spike was uncalled for and now a man is dead. Warmth spreads over my leg, and I pivot to see Sable's hand resting on my thigh. I look up into his green eyes. A girl could get lost in their depths all too easily.

"I'm sorry for what Spike did to your friend. But please stop blaming yourself *and me*... for *his* actions." He grasps my chin before I can turn away. "You deserve a life without having to barter and beg for the essentials."

"What do you think, Sara?" Celeste asks.

"It's beautiful."

We all pile out and head towards the log cabin in front of us.

"Why don't you guys stay by the car. I won't be long." Celeste smiles.

Sara hugs me. "Please make sure you visit."

"I promise I'll visit often."

"Sara, Ms. Debbie will be more than happy to let you call Scarlett," Sable inserts as he leans against the car.

Sara flings herself on him and squeezes. "Thanks for rescuing us." As he rubs her back, she whispers, "And make sure she stays away from Spike—he isn't very nice to her." She pivots before skipping inside the house to meet her new family. My heart aches at the realization. Will she even *want* to see me anymore? But I shake my head of those selfish thoughts. Sara will be well taken care of, even if I'm not in her life.

"Are you certain she'll be safe here?" I turn to Sable.

"Yes, this land is guarded by a strong pack, and we have asked them to watch over her as a favor to us."

"Wait… you said another pack?" I squeak out. "How many are there?"

"Just think of a pack… as a family. That's how many."

"And the Native Americans who live here, they don't mind?"

"These wolves and the natives have always coexisted. Some even say that's how this pack became so powerful, because of the human presence and protection."

I lean on the car next to Sable, while I pray that Sara settles in well with this family. Out of the corner of my eye, I spot a man and woman appear from the dense darkness of the forest.

Sable lifts his hand in greeting. "Well, look who showed up, brother."

Aspen glances up from his phone and smiles before the group embraces. Then they turn their attention to me. "Scarlett, this is Frost and Raven. They're the alphas of the Tala pack; they watch over this area."

I nod an acknowledgment and return my attention to the house as Celeste saunters over to join us. "Sara is settling in nicely, Scarlett. She promises to call you tonight with all the details. Frost! Raven! How lovely to see you both. This is Scarlett, the young woman I was telling you about."

Raven steps closer, mere inches from my face, and looks into my eyes. Are all shifters this... *friendly*?

"They said your name is Scarlett?"

I shuffle back from the crazy lady. "Yes."

Raven turns to Frost as tears shimmer in her eyes. Then the intimidating alpha strides over, and I swallow. This man is tall, with a commanding presence that seems to radiate from him. Add in the stern look and no-fucks-given attitude, and the tension is suffocating. He takes a deep breath and closes his eyes before they shoot back open, and the two newcomers embrace me.

My pupils dilate and I attempt to garner Sable's attention. But he and his mom are sharing an animated exchange. As if he can feel my glare, he cranes his head in my direction.

"I'm sorry, but I don't, um, hug much," I sputter to the overly affectionate shifters.

They pull away. "I'm sorry... we just... It's been so long since..." Raven's words sob out, and Frost holds her.

"Why don't we have some lunch?" Celeste guides our group (me included) into the woods.

This situation is super awkward, and I feel like I'm missing something big. "What was that about? Are they always so touchy when they meet new people?"

"It's a long story."

"Oh?"

"But it's not mine to tell, sweetie. Otherwise, I would. But I promise you no harm will come to you. They are good people."

I yelp as Aspen gallops past us in his wolf form. I can't help the giggle that escapes as his tongue hangs out and his bushy tail swishes wildly. He looks so happy.

"You can join him if you want, guys. I don't mind walking."

Sable grins as he sheds his clothes and grows fur. And just when I think he's going to take off towards Aspen, he head-butts the underside of my knees. I fall backwards, but he pushes his muzzle between my legs and nudges me towards his shoulder blades. Before I can jump down, he bullets forward. I scream and grab fistfuls of fur, holding on for dear life. Once I'm used to the rhythm of his movements, I peek above his head and watch as he nears Aspen's rear. Sable nips at his brother's heels playfully. Aspen steals a glance behind him, then lowers his ears and speeds up. And I laugh as the wind whips through our hair. Can life get any better than this?

As we approach the end of the tree line, the woodlands open to a valley, and in the center is a glimmering stream. I skim my surroundings and see cave homes littering the corners and wolves and humans working around the area. The wind tosses my unruly hair, and pack members turn in my direction. My face heats as soon as their eyes fall on me. They rush over, but Sable's hackles rise and he steps back.

Frost holds up a hand to the approaching group before he ushers us into the brightest cave. "I'm sorry about that. They're always hesitant when it comes to outsiders."

"They seemed more excited than worried," I add as I climb off Sable and Celeste offers him clothes.

Frost smirks at my observation. "I doubt much escapes you, Little Wolf."

My blood runs cold and my head shoots up. "What did you call me?"

"I'm sorry… Do you find that offensive?"

"It… uh…" I flounder, trying to find the right words, as memories of Spike begin to assault my sensibilities. Is this an omen? Does Frost know about the Fangs?

I sway, but Sable grabs my waist before I fall. "Do you need some air?"

"Please."

He helps me outside, his hold firm. "You were off in your head. Is everything okay?"

His question is not an easy one to answer, and I don't know how much to tell him. "No. It's not. Nothing is okay. Spike… he… I… It's just everything, all right? It's all too much, too quick. First, I'm proposed to by somebody old enough to be my father, then I almost die twice and have to watch as my friend's murdered. And now… now, I'm falling in love with a crazy wolfman!" The confessions tumble out all at once. I clamp a hand over my mouth and groan, before retreating to the other side of the cave's exterior and kicking the stone.

I'm such an idiot. What was I thinking? Sable is a super-human wolf creature; he would never look my way. Not like that. I bet it's even against their rules! And yet…

I can't help but feel this pull towards him. He's fun, caring, protective… and nothing that I deserve.

When Sable approaches, I clear my throat and try to ignore the fact that I just professed my love for a man who is still practically a stranger, and instead shift the conversation to something less embarrassing. "Spike's nickname for me was Little Wolf. When Frost called me that, it brought back memories. Memories I would rather not think about right now."

"Wait, how do *you* know Spike?" I pivot towards the speaker and see Frost approaching us.

"It's a long, *personal* story."

Frost opens his mouth, likely to press for more details, but he's cut off when we all hear a commotion near the edge of the woods. "Alpha, we have an intruder in the east quadrant," a male reports from across the field.

Frost's gaze narrows as he strides past us and towards the intruder. My own eyes widen with recognition. "Freddy?" I whisper. The towering figure tilts his head and glares back at me.

"You *know* this man?" Frost prompts.

"Not only does she know me, old man, but she is also coming back with me. She's Spike's mate and doesn't belong here any more than I do."

I can't control the terror as it turns my blood cold. This can't be happening. Sable steadies me, placing a comforting hand on the small of my back. "Don't worry. We won't let him take you."

Frost draws his dagger as he stalks towards Freddy. "I should cut your tongue out for such lies."

"It's the truth. That's why she was lost in the woods. It was the day we had our ancestral gathering. She drank of the ceremonial wine, and Spike asked for her hand."

Sable's touch encourages me to fight. "I never agreed to marry that son of a bitch. *He* asked, and *I* said no."

"She's a filthy liar! I heard her agree. And then, when Spike walked away to tend to an emergency, she ran off into the woods— *drunk*."

Frost points the dagger at the man's chest. "Don't you dare speak about my daughter like that, you ingrate. If she says she didn't agree to his proposal, that's exactly what happened. Now leave."

Wait... daughter? Is he lying to protect me? Are alphas allowed to do that? Or is the term meant to be more symbolic? As in, she's *like a daughter* to me...

"Even if she didn't agree, she has slept with him numerous times."

My face turns red and I can feel the weight of everyone's gaze.

"We are not speaking of lost virtues here, boy. We are talking about marriage proposals and pack members. My daughter never agreed to be his mate. Now turn around and walk out. Jackson." A man steps out of the shadows and nods. "Follow him. Ensure he makes it home."

Freddy strides off, issuing a warning to the open air. "This isn't over."

Once they're out of earshot, Frost turns his glare on me. "Why the *hell* would you sleep with that trash?"

I blink at his grating tone, but recover quickly. "*Excuse* me? You have no right to talk to me like that."

"I have every right to talk to you like that. You *are* my daughter."

"Have you *lost* your mind? My piss-poor excuse for a father dumped me on the side of the road when I was three!"

With wild eyes, Frost swings his dagger across my chest. I step back, waiting for the inevitable bite of the blade, but it doesn't come. Instead, my shredded sweater flutters to the ground, leaving me in my dingy camisole.

"Look at her back, Sable, and inform her just how wrong she is. She may not trust her father's word, but I know she'll believe yours," Frost booms; his voice vibrates from the base of my toes to the top of my spine, causing Sable to immediately comply. "What do you see, boy?"

Sable runs his warm fingertip across my right shoulder blade. "It's very faint, but there's a crescent moon with the letters F and R."

All around us, the growing crowd gasps and points. I reach back to where Sable is indicating. "What are you talking about? I don't have any tattoos."

"It's *not* a tattoo, but a birthmark, granted to us by Luna in order to identify parentage." He sheaths his dagger. "Do you trust the boy, or should we take a photo for you?"

The revelation has my head spinning. Frost is my father? I take in his stature, then Raven's. They look nothing like me. Sable misinterprets my silence as a plea for more evidence and snaps a picture with his phone. He hands me the device while staring at me in a new light. *In awe.* I can only gawk at the image, unsure as to what I'm actually seeing, until Sable sharpens the icon while zooming in.

I swallow down my lump and force myself to look at the coward *claiming* to be my father. After all these years, I can finally let him have it! "You abandoned me."

Frost appears taken aback. "No, I didn't. You were abducted. You ran to grab a toy in the woods while we were cooking dinner, and when you didn't return, we came to get you. But we only found…" He swallows. "We found my brother… dead. We assumed he must have followed you and was attacked… We searched high and low, but we never found you."

"That can't be *true*. The orphanage said a police officer found me wandering in the woods. *Alone*." I fight my own twitching lips. Sable rubs my back, and I can't help but melt into his chest to hide my tears. Can this be true? Were they really looking for me? After all this time, what does everything mean?

"Why don't we go inside, where it's warmer?" Sable suggests. I lean on him as we walk back to the house. Once we're situated, Raven serves us coffee and biscuits. I stare at the liquid as steam escapes, wishing for more answers but receiving none.

"We love you very much. We never stopped searching," Raven soothes.

"Then why didn't you find me? I was in Carson City. Surely you checked there."

"Of course we did. But we were looking for a three-year-old… with white hair and amber eyes."

I run my hand through my crimson locks. "They didn't know my name, so the kids called me Scarlett, because of the color," I say more to myself than anyone else.

Raven grabs my hands in hers, and I meet her tear-filled eyes. "I swear to you, we'll figure out what happened. But you… you *are* our daughter. Even though the birthmark is faded, it doesn't lie."

There is a knock on the door, and an older woman pads in with the help of a walking stick. Her fading amber eyes crinkle as she smiles at me. "Oh, my! And here I thought I would be worm food before I saw my grandbaby again." She embraces me in a surprisingly strong hold, then sits down with a huff. "I'm getting too old for this shifting crap, Frost. What is it that you need from me?"

"You recognized Maya, Mom?" Frost stutters out.

"Of course I did, you lemonhead. I may not see or hear all that well, but I sure as hell can smell better than anyone around. And that scent belongs to my dear grandbaby."

"But, Mom, she doesn't look like Maya. She has red hair and green eyes."

The old woman leans closer, her nose touching mine. "Well, I'll be damned. She does look a little different." She shrugs and sits back. When she notices Sable, she grins. "And she found herself a hot potato too."

"Mom. Please. Have you heard of anything that can change a shifter's appearance like this? We need to know why Maya looks different, and why she can't shift into her wolf form."

"Well, of course she can shift. Can't you?"

"No. I didn't even know it was a possibility."

The old lady leans back again and scratches her chin.

"What are you thinking, Mom?"

"It's a *long* shot, but when I was a pup, my gammy told me this fairy tale. It was about an ancient native, who placed an enchantment on his lover. He wanted to *sneak* her away without any shifters suspecting, so they could be together."

"What happened to them?" Frost inquires.

"Well, I suppose they lived happily ever after."

"But how did they change her *back* to her old self?"

"The legend said that once the couple made it to safety, they kissed and the spell was broken. And she returned to her true form."

I can't help the laugh that bursts forth. "Oh, *please*. Give me a break. That sounds like *Cinderella*."

"You mean *Sleeping Beauty*," the old woman corrects.

"Whoever it is! There's *no* way that can be true."

The old woman laughs and slaps her knee. "She's definitely our kin, Frost. She's as stubborn as a mule."

I frown. "I'm only speaking logically here."

"Logic? *Really*? We're shapeshifters. Nothing about us is logical." Everybody sips their coffee to hide their snickers. I roll my eyes and taste the charcoal liquid. "So, what are you waiting for? I'm not going to live forever."

"What do you mean?"

"Kiss the handsome prince already!"

I cough on my biscuit. "Excuse me?"

"Get to it. We've waited fifteen years to see our baby's face."

"But *the prince* didn't alter my appearance to begin with. Wouldn't that have something to do with your hypothesis? The same man who enchanted the girl also *kissed* her—or so your story goes."

"What's the harm in trying? Best-case scenario, you can shift and return to your natural state. Worst case, you stay as you are and have an excuse to kiss a hunk."

I hold back a smirk. I like her spirit. I side-glance Sable, then look at each set of eyes fixated on us. "If you all expect me to do this, could I at least get some privacy." They slowly trickle into the living room, leaving Sable and me alone. I clear my throat as I wrap my fingertips around my mug. "Listen, I know this is awkward. You don't have to do this if you don't want to. I know it's a lot of pressure, and—"

My heart stops as he trails his hands over the sides of my face. Then his thumbs brush my cheeks softly. "Are you sure this is what *you* want, Scarlett?"

My brain hurts. It's hard to think. Do I want to become Maya Tala? Or stay Scarlett nobody? My eyes meet Sable's, and I can't help but melt as the realization hits me: it doesn't matter who I am, as long as Sable is by my side. Ever since we met, it has been a whirlwind of occurrences, but for the most part, I've never felt *more* whole. Like a piece of me was missing, and now I've found it. However, is he my happily ever after?

There's only one way to find out. "Yes, I do want to do this. Kiss me, Sable."

He doesn't even think twice as he tugs me to him and leans down. When our lips touch, a flame ignites in my chest and it slowly burns throughout my every nerve ending. My heart is pounding so fast I'm sure it can be heard for miles. No man has ever treated me the way he has, with such compassion and tenderness. I feel like I could stand here forever, wrapped in the safety of his arms.

"Scarlett, open your eyes for me." My lashes flutter in response. "I'll be damned. The old lady isn't as crazy as she looks."

"You mean, it actually worked?" I run my fingertips over my face. I don't *feel* any different. Everybody crowds back in, separating Sable and me.

"My baby girl has finally come home to us." Raven envelops me in her arms.

Frost joins our embrace. "We are so glad to have you back,

Maya." He pulls away and watches me for a second. "Unless you would prefer that we call you Scarlett?"

Although *family* isn't a word in my vocabulary, I'm excited to define it… in time. I pivot to make eye contact with everyone around me. I smile as a tear slips down my cheek. When did my luck *change*? "No, Maya is just fine."

Sable

Games

The moment I see Frost and Raven leave their territory, I know something is wrong. I plaster on my best fake-ass smile and shake hands with the alpha, but I know it doesn't fool him as he squeezes harder than necessary in return. When they approach Scarlett, I fight every urge to jump in their path and claim her as mine. No way are they getting their claws into her. She belongs to *our* pack. It's not official yet, but it will be… as soon as I can convince her to break ties with Carson City.

"Wait, Sable. Give them a minute." My mom snatches my wrist.

I tear my hand away. "What is this? Did you do this?" I can't stop the agony from lacing my accusation—she knows how I feel about *them*. The memories break through my barrier as I fight the whirlwind of emotions…

"Frost, please!

"I appreciate your loyalty but don't cross the line, boy. My word is final."

"Fuck that!" I shout as my fists itch to meet his jaw.

The large man steps towards me, ready to pounce. "What?"

"You can't just give up on Maya!"

"Honey, we will never give up. But we can't possibly ask the pack to continue this tedious search; they are wearing thin." Raven tries to soothe my nerves. "We will never completely stop looking, but we need to space out our excursions. Please understand that, Sable."

"Have you asked the members? I know they will continue at this pace, if you asked them. Please, Raven!" I focus my attention on her, hoping to speak to her maternal instincts.

"Enough!" Frost stands in front of his wife.

I know I shouldn't, but I can't stop myself. My fist collides with his jaw; my hand throbs as I eagerly wait for the inevitable retaliation.

Raven squeaks but Frost holds his arm out, stopping her approach. Then he narrows his eyes at me. "This is the only time I'll let this go. Because I know how distraught you are. But pull that shit again, and I'll ban you from ever stepping a paw in this territory."

"Fuck this place!" I roar. "Mark my words, I'll never forgive you for this! Never!"

"Sable, they just want to greet her." My mom tugs me back to the present. I grind my teeth as I watch their interactions. This is bullshit. They are up to something.

When they embrace her, I all but spit fire. My head shoots to my mom. "What the fuck is this?"

"Calm down."

"Why are they touching her!"

"They think she is their lost daughter."

The statement slams into my gut. I take in Scarlett's appearance. "Impossible."

The rest of my mom's words are drowned out as she guides us through the forest and into Tala territory. I drag my feet, knowing I'm not welcomed there. But when Scarlett warms my arm with her proximity while staying far away from Frost and Raven, I can't help the grin I flash them. *Suck on that!* The glare from Frost is worth everything.

When Aspen shifts and takes off, an idea pings in my head. Throwing a quick smirk in the alpha's direction, I shed my clothes and morph into a furry beast. I push out my chest and prance around Scarlett. Frost gives me his signature *don't even think about it* face. But I shove my head between her legs until she falls back and grips my fur tightly. Then, as quick as lightening, I hurtle towards my brother. Her squeal of excitement does amazing things to me. I could listen to it all day long. I love how happy she is, just being with me.

"Try to keep up, old man, or I may steal her from you," Aspen taunts.

A growl rips through my throat as I snap at his back legs. *"You're just lucky I have her on my back, or you'd be dead."*

He turns a grin my way before taking off. As we come together with the Tala pack, the tension looms between us. I rarely show my face here. But everything changes when Scarlett admits she is falling for me, and I see the birthmark on her shoulder. Then, when she just laughs the story off, my face falls. And I zone out, trying to understand it all. Could Scarlett be Maya? Is that why my wolf stirs in her presence?

Suddenly, she clears her throat as she squeezes her mug and offers me *an out*. Her embarrassment is hot. Doesn't she realize I don't give a shit about the others watching me when I claim her? I'd spread her on the table and lick every inch of her if I could. But I'll take what I can get...

My huge hands easily cup her face, though her hesitation worries me. If I'm doing this, she needs to be *all* in, because she'll never touch another man. She'll finally be with her true mate. Forever. "Are you sure this is what *you* want, Scarlett?"

I almost lose hope, but then she whispers, "Yes, I do want to do this. Kiss me, Sable."

I slam my lips to hers, and I know my life will never be the same. It's not a *come in your pants* kind of moment, but there sure as hell are promises of that in the very near future. My wolf purrs as I continue to claim her mouth with mine. Damn, it feels good. She tastes like the sweetest honey, and I can't wait to strip her down. To bring her every fantasy to life.

Scarlett is my mate. I've finally found her. And now she is safe, in my arms. But is Scarlett really Maya? Was the fable true? I force myself to take a step back. "Scarlett, open your eyes for me. I'll be damned. The old lady isn't as crazy as she looks."

Her family pushes me aside as they welcome her. Although it makes me madder than a rabid dog, I know where she'll end up. It's inevitable. Let them have *this* moment. Those to come are all mine.

As she's introduced to the rest of the pack with Raven, Frost corners me. "Regret not looking harder? Don't worry, you don't have to admit that I was right and you were wrong." I pat his shoulder. "Because it goes without saying."

"This changes nothing."

"Of course it does. Because although *we* have beef, we also have a common interest in protecting her."

Frost's sneer makes me cringe as he replies, "So, when are you moving in?"

"Me? Technically, she is my mate, which means she gets to live on my turf."

"We will see." I roll my eyes in response (because I won't fight over something I know as fact) and stride towards my future wife, but he slams me against the cave wall with a growl. "She is all I have."

I thump my hands against his chest. "Fuck you! Now… *now*, you want to be a part of her life? What about all those years I begged you to look for her?"

"We never stopped looking!" he roars.

"And when I went to the Guardian to ask for assistance? You wouldn't lift a paw to accompany me!" We continue to stare each other down.

"We will just have to agree to *disagree*." Frost straightens and pivots, but before he walks off, he throws over his shoulder, "Remember, Sable, we both love her and if *either* of us pulls too hard, she will run. And we will *both* lose."

Scarlett

Tala Pack

Once they retell our family history, I explain how I've been surviving in Carson City. Even though they keep silent, it's not hard to feel the heat radiating off them. Blood will be spilled over my mistreatment—who will be the victor has yet to be determined. The Tala pack may be powerful, but I have witnessed Spike's viciousness firsthand and it's difficult to imagine how they'd survive his cruelty.

After a cozy family dinner and meeting the rest of the pack, I look forward to a little peace and quiet. I slip through the crowd until I reach the edge of the stream. I listen to the water as it glimmers in the moonlight. Then I snatch a river stone and run the cold rock through my hands before chucking it. The ripples start off small and then fan out to my feet. Everything is changing so fast, and I am finding it difficult to breathe. I never knew having a family would be this exhausting, both mentally and physically.

"I knew I'd find you here." Sable sidles up beside me. I enjoy his presence as we giggle at the waddling geese. My head falls on his shoulder and soaks in his strength. How I caught the attention of this wolfman is beyond me, but I'm not complaining. He wraps an arm around my waist. "Just so you know, when I see Spike, I'm going to rip his head off."

"You'll need to get in line. There are a lot of us gearing up for that task," Dad interjects from behind us. "I can't wait to sink my *fangs* into him."

"Does shifting hurt?" I ask to no one in particular, rubbing my canines with the tip of my finger.

"It feels awkward at first, but it doesn't cause any pain," Sable replies. "You just think about changing, and it happens. Don't worry, you'll do great, and you'll love it. It's the best feeling in the world: running through the woods, at full speed, with your tongue out and the wind whipping against your fur." His eyes give off a faraway look, like he's reliving the experience. I glance to my dad and he too is lost in thought. My heartbeat quickens as I consider the possibility of shifting and the freedom that follows.

"Sable, honey, we are going to head out now. I have an early appointment tomorrow. Plus, Sky isn't answering her phone so I'm going to stop by the steakhouse and give her an earful," Celeste announces as she and Aspen join us.

"I'm sure she just got wrapped up in paperwork again," Aspen grumbles. "Good night, Maya. Sable, are you coming back with us?"

Sable shrugs and turns to me. "Do you want me to stay with you?"

"I'm sure you have better things to do than sit here and listen to me moan and complain."

"I enjoy being with you."

"Sable, you're welcome to sleep in our *guest* room." I smirk at my dad's tone. It will take time to get used to a protective parent, particularly one who can shift and rip your limbs off before you can scream.

"You don't have to worry about me, Sable. I've been on my own this whole time."

"I understand you don't need me by your side. But I do look forward to the day when you'll *want* me there." He brushes his lips against my neck. The way he whispers sends warm shivers down to my toes. Sable tugs me into an embrace, and I wrap my arms around him and take in his scent. It's soft and woodsy, with a hint of fallen leaves and fresh soil. I purr against his warm chest, regretting not asking him to stay, as images of us rolling around under the covers play in my mind. I blink and pull back. Where did that come from? So many of my emotions are heightened including my *desire*.

"Don't be afraid of your new gifts. They are there to aid you in all you do, especially when you shift and hunt." A wild look crosses his face. "It's exhilarating… the thrill of the chase."

I swallow and my face flushes as I realize he isn't talking about deer.

"Well, I think it's about time you travel home." Dad pats Sable's back, and I feel the weight of his tone. From what was explained to me, an alpha's word holds power and you don't disobey.

Sable kisses my lips softly, and when he stops, I sway. How do I get used to this influx of hormones? Stupid wolf powers. All I want is to bury him inside me.

"I need to go into the shop for a few hours, but I'll be back as soon as I can." Sable kisses my palm. "I'm counting the minutes until we are together again."

I press up on my tiptoes and kiss his cheek. Then I whisper into his ear, "Hurry back."

With what seems to be much effort, he walks into the woods and towards their car. As I watch him disappear, I feel as if my heart is being torn from my rib cage.

"It's hard saying goodbye to our mates. But don't worry, once you have settled here, you and Sable can join hands in marriage and start your new lives together."

"Oh, I never said anything about *marrying* anybody."

Dad guides me into the cave home, places a mug of hot chocolate in my hands, and sits on the other side of the table. "Trust me, I'm in no rush to see my only daughter get married."

Raven offers some warm peanut butter cookies and sits beside me. "He's right. It's so good to finally have you home. I don't want to rush you leaving us."

"I'm in no rush to leave either. Dad, you said that Sable was my *mate*. What did you mean by that?"

"Well, the Canis family was part of our pack before they branched off and started their own." He smiles sadly. "It's difficult for a pack to have numerous males because it can result in fighting, and on occasion, death. It's tough for our inner wolves to understand our human need to stay together, because it views other alpha males as a threat."

I allow him a moment to collect his thoughts as pain flashes across his face. I reach over and touch his hand. "Earlier… you mentioned how you killed Spike's brother. Is that what happened between you two? Your wolves fought for the position of alpha?"

"Spike's brother, Mark, was power hungry, and I thought—having learned from our past entanglements—that he would finally move on and give up. But one night, he hid in some underbrush on the boundary of our territory and ambushed me." He rubs a scar on his neck. "I only defended myself, but in the end, he lay dead at my feet. Spike was beside himself with anger." He shakes his head. "I don't think he ever grieved for his brother. He only sought out vengeance, and it grew into resentment. That's why after you went missing, he was the first person we hunted down."

"I'm sorry, but his death is not your fault. You know that, right?"

"Enough of this talk. You asked about mates, and I got sidetracked. Phoenix was my beta before he requested to leave the pack. He was my best friend and second in command. Well, when the Canis family decided to branch out, they made a peace pact with us. It stated that if our first-borns found favor towards each other and Luna blessed the union, they would marry and take over as alphas here one day."

"Is that why I feel a connection to him?"

"That is between you and Luna, my dear. Because she predestines our future spouses. But as you shift and allow your wolf and human senses to comingle, you will feel stronger connections to the world in general." Raven smiles at me. "I know it's a lot to take in, but it will become second nature. In time."

We continue to discuss the significant roles an alpha plays, and how my actions will be highly scrutinized by other pack members because of this responsibility. I can't suppress my groan as I recall all the things I've done in Carson City and wonder if my past will continue to haunt me now. "Dad, I stole to survive when I left the orphanage, and I'm wanted by every cop in the city. Maybe me being next in line isn't a great idea."

"Nonsense, you are a *new* woman, Maya." He shrugs. "If I need to pay off a few cops, I can." His comment stings—it reminds me of Spike.

"I'm the same person."

"Your hair and eyes say differently, dear." Raven winks.

I stand up and shake my head. "I need to be held accountable for my actions, just like everybody else."

"But, honey, you did it to stay alive."

"Yes, and so does every other homeless man and woman in that rundown city." The silence is suffocating. But I refuse to back down. I knowingly stole and should be punished for my crimes, even if my doing so meant I could eat.

"You know what? I'm exhausted. Why don't we head to bed? It's getting pretty late." Raven guides me to the bedrooms down the hall. "We left your room untouched. But feel free to rearrange it as you see fit."

I can't help but cringe as I'm bombarded by every shade of *pink* imaginable. But when I turn to my mom, my sarcastic retort falters as I see her wet cheeks. She collects me in yet another hug and sobs. Treading in new territory, and uncertain what the familial protocol is when comforting a parent, I remember what Sable did for me and I rub my palm over her back.

A pretty pink princess doesn't have *anything* on me. But the room is more than I could have ever imagined. All this *belongs* to me. These stuffed animals, this bed, and everything inside. Mine. I'm almost nineteen years old, and I finally own *something*. And my heart is bursting.

I trail my fingertips over the smooth bubblegum-shaded comforter. Okay, so the color isn't *that* awful. I glance at the vanity, adorned with picture frames, and the one closest to me catches my attention. I lift it to get a better look.

"Now, that was a great day. It was your very *first* birthday." Raven bites her trembling lip. "Your father planned this huge event. And… it got rained out." She laughs. "But the pack came together and set up canopies, then we all celebrated well into the night."

I lift another frame and tilt my head at the little boy's smiling face. "Is this Sable?"

"I haven't seen this picture in ages. Even though his family moved off the reserve, they still make it to all of our gatherings. My, he looks so young and carefree here, doesn't he? And that boy was always so protective over you, even at a young age. He will make a great father one day."

I frown, the question eating away at my subconscious. "If Sable was so protective, what happened when I was abducted?"

"It was a very hard time for us all. We searched everywhere for you. Sable closed himself off from everybody and everything." She swipes at the corner of her eye. "He even traveled to the Guardians, seeking their assistance to find you. It took months to hunt them down, but in the end, they decided not to step in. It broke the poor boy. He said if the Guardians refused to help, it probably meant…" She chokes on a sob. "…that you were dead."

Everybody thought I was dead. For years, I've been so mad at them for abandoning me. But I had no idea they went through all of this just to find me. Especially Sable. His obvious loyalty brings tears to my eyes. "Who are the Guardians? Do they really have the ability to locate someone in that manner—someone no one else can find?"

"The Guardians are Luna's helpers in our realm, while she rules from above. The legends vary: who they are and what they can do. We have never personally witnessed their feats, but some say that they each hold an elemental power and are part of Luna's original creations. Their sole purpose is to keep peace between packs and humans. They only intervene when needed—which, in my experience, is very rarely."

I shake my aching head. Now there are mystical beings involved? What the hell kind of world am I really living in? And here I thought the worst thing to happen to someone was freezing to death or starvation. Now we have neck-breaking shifters and power-wielding deities. "Are the Guardians shifters too?"

"I don't know for certain if they are. I can only tell you what's been passed down: the belief that they can take any form."

"Any form?" I squeak out. This world is getting darker by the minute. I clamp my mouth shut. *No more questions.* Because the answers are just making everything worse.

I feel my mom's hand on my back, and I look into her eyes. "Don't fret over all of this, sweetheart. Luna brought you back to us, and we'll protect you always and forever."

We pivot as we hear footsteps approaching and see Dad and his beta, Jackson. "We have a situation that has arisen," Dad announces. The hairs on my arm stick up at his militant tone. "The Canis family hasn't been able to track down their daughter, Sky. They went to her place of occupation and all of her employees said she went home for the day, hours ago, but her car is still at the restaurant with her belongings inside."

Scarlett

Life for a Life

I jump out of the car and search the perimeter of the steakhouse. It's clean, with a log cabin feel, and nestled near the Canis family woodlands. I take in the crisp night air. But nothing calms the anxiety building in my chest.

"I told you to wait in the car," Dad grumbles. "I just got you back. I don't need you getting hurt."

"You can't shut me in a bubble. I'm a big girl."

"Thank you for coming so quickly." Phoenix embraces my dad as he would a brother.

"What do we know?" Dad demands.

"We are reviewing the security footage, but it's not helping. The video shows her grabbing her belongings and walking out towards the parking lot."

"Where is her car?" I ask.

"Just over here, in the corner, where all the employees park."

"There are no cameras in the vicinity?" I glance around the well-lit area near the back entrance.

"No."

I sweep through the location, but nothing's out of place. The others are in a heated discussion about calling the cops or waiting a little longer. I rub my temples, trying to figure out what to do next. Then an idea hits me. No… Surely they wouldn't?

But maybe they did. "Tell me how to shift." All eyes turn to me. "If I can sniff around the area, maybe I can pick up a familiar scent."

"I appreciate the help, but we have done that already. The scents are of the employees and a few regular customers—nothing else."

I rub my chin as my mind works overtime.

"What are you thinking, Maya?" Dad probes.

"I know Spike's pack like the back of my hand. If I can access my new abilities and my senses really are *that* good, I can possibly narrow down the search. Or I won't find anything out of the ordinary, and it will just be a waste of time."

The men exchange a glance, and my dad shrugs. "It couldn't hurt. But you've never shifted before. Are you sure about this?"

"If it helps get Sky back, absolutely." I glance around. "Maybe I could shift in the car though? That way I, uh, don't walk around undressed in front of everybody."

They chuckle before Phoenix clears his throat to try to ease my scowling face. "My vehicle is the biggest. Let me pull it around for you."

Once he strides off, Dad pats my shoulder and the pride in his voice lifts the butterflies from my stomach. "Thank you."

I can only nod as I fight back my emotions. Once inside the car, I disrobe. I wrap my arms around myself to alleviate the chill. But insecurity envelops my heart. What if I can't do this? What if I fail and Sky dies?

A knock sounds on the window, and I yelp. When I turn, I see Sable's back to the glass. "Stop overthinking this. Just take a deep breath and allow your wolf to come through."

"What do you think I've been doing in here? It's easier said than done."

"Wow. I never took you for a coward."

"What did you just call me?"

"You heard me. Now, we're losing light fast. So, man up and get your ass out here."

I clench my jaw. That little jerk! Here I am, doing him a favor and… I smirk. He is baiting me. I take a deep breath and imagine a big, hairy wolf. I open my eyes and frown at my hands. "Sable, I am broken."

"Don't give up. Try again."

"That's the *best* advice you have?"

"Yup." I imagine Wolfie's smug face. I chuckle as I recall the fish he flopped at me when I was starving. And his whimper as he lay in the trap. The back door swings open, and I look up into Sable's eyes. "So, how does it feel?"

I glance at my paw and bark. I am covered in white fur!

"Now, *very slowly*, step out. Four paws are more complicated than two feet."

Excitement bubbles in my throat as I feel lighter, stronger, and *freer*. My tail wags, hitting the back seats. Sable grins before he steps aside so I can jump out. I wince at the distance. I can do this. I put one paw out but stumble head over feet until I crash into the gravel.

"Maybe this was a bad idea," Dad announces.

I stand shakily on all fours. How the heck do dogs do this? I put one foot in front of the other, again and again, until I'm more confident. Then I pick up the pace to just above a snail's crawl. Soon, I'm leaping around the parking lot, enjoying the wind in my face.

I hear Sable chuckle, and I'm reminded of the small crowd. "She's acting like a pup. You would never guess she's a full-grown adult, on a mission." I jump into his arms, and we thump to the ground. He clutches on to me and takes the blow without hesitation. When he moans, I lick his face excitedly. Then his warm hands travel all across my fur, and I can't suppress my purr. "You are absolutely breathtaking. In *both* forms."

My dad ruins the moment by clearing his throat. "Maya, we need you to control your wolf and focus on the task at hand. I promise you'll have plenty of time to play... *later*."

I prance over to Sky's car and sniff the tires. I definitely smell her, but there's another familiar scent too.

"Take your time and move around. Your wolf will do the rest."

My ears prick as the odor registers. I bark, trying to relay my findings. Dad opens the car door and I hop inside. Then I shift back and throw my clothes on. I stumble out of the car again as I try to adjust to two feet. "I know who was with her when she came back to her car. It was one of the Fangs—Freddy. You met him earlier. Charming little douchebag."

"Are you absolutely sure?" Dad urges.

Before I can confirm my findings, Aspen walks around the corner. "Maya is right. It's the Fangs. Spike just called Mom."

Phoenix balls his fists. "What did he say?"

"He said he will hand over Sky, without bloodshed, under *one* condition." We all watch as he wrings his hands together. Then his eyes meet mine, and my heart sinks before the words leave his mouth. "Spike wants Maya in exchange."

My dad and Sable stand in front of me, to form a protective barrier, but I push them aside. "We need to think clearly here. Spike won't hesitate to kill Sky if he thinks we aren't going to comply. I need to return, so we can get her back unharmed."

"Like hell you are." Sable grabs my wrist. "We will get Sky back another way. A way that doesn't require a sacrifice." I know this is hard for him. His sister is in danger, but he doesn't want to get her back at my expense. It's a lose-lose situation. I see the confusion etched on his face, even if he tries to hide it. But I've already made up my mind. "Maya, we do not trade a life for a life. We will gather our neighboring packs and demand Sky's safe return. End of story."

Everybody saunters towards the restaurant, while I linger behind with Aspen. He side-glances me and I can tell he doesn't agree with their plan either. So I use this to my advantage and whisper to him, "This plan is too dangerous, Aspen. Far more is at risk than a single life."

"But they are right. We can't trade your life for Sky's."

"I can handle myself. But Sky, she has always had everything done for her. I don't think she'll survive. And that's if Spike doesn't kill her out of spite. We need to try to find a way around this."

"If you can meet me at the edge of the reserve, I can drive you to

Carson City. Then I can wait for Sky's release and bring her home."

"Are you sure, Aspen? There will be consequences... for both of us."

He looks towards our families, then back to me. "Only if you are still willing to go through with this. I would never force you."

I rub my arms as I watch my parents and Sable. Am I willing to give them up to save somebody I barely know? Sable pivots to me and winks before he's pulled back into the conversation. Losing me crushed him the first time. Would it happen again? Or would losing his sister throw him over the edge and hurt him beyond repair? "Let's sleep on it, Aspen. If they can't figure out something soon, then it will be up to us to make it happen."

I stab at my steak as we all sit inside the restaurant. The food is delicious, but my stomach is in knots.

"I know what you're planning," Sable whispers to me. "I heard you and Aspen talking. You both are idiots if you think we can't hear you from five feet away. Your dad has already implemented guards on the borders to make sure you can't go through with your crazy plan."

"How can you say that? Your sister is in trouble."

He grabs my chin. "I'm concerned about her, but Sky is strong. Please have more faith in the packs."

I pull my face away. "I don't want anybody else getting hurt. Especially when I can just turn myself in. Trust me, Spike won't stop until he gets what he wants." I push out my chair and stomp into the cold night air. I lean on the railing, watching a pair of deer as they search the ground in the dark woods. I start when a warm body comes up behind me. Sable lowers his lips to my neck before breathing in my scent. I soak in his passion and turn around to wrap my arms over his neck. We hold each other and sway to the night's sweet symphony.

"I can't lose you again." he whispers before nibbling my ear. "I need you… more than you know."

The door slams open behind us. "That bastard! I'm going to slice him from head to toe!" My dad growls as he shifts; his clothes float in pieces to the ground before he gallops off with a howl to the moon. Raven rushes over, but she's too late.

"Mom, what's going on?"

"Spike's pack took two more shifters, and your father is blaming himself for not protecting them."

"Did anyone get hurt?"

"Yes, but they do not have life-threatening injuries." She watches me carefully. "Everything will be fine, sweetheart. You'll see."

"This is ridiculous! You are both blinded by your love for me. Everybody is!" I'm done doing what's expected of me. I leap over the railing and follow my dad's example. I shift mid-stride while shredding my clothes. Then I gallop as fast and far as I can. My life is not worth it. I need to turn myself in before it's too late for her.

My nose and ears work in harmony as I determine where to go. And soon, I'm beyond exhausted on the edge of Carson City. I let out a relieved sigh when I don't hear anybody following me. I stick to the familiar shadows as I make my way towards the Warehouse. Once I'm close, I shift back and climb the fire escape that leads to Spike's loft. I steady myself against the wall and place my ear to the door. Taking a deep breath, I inch the door open, but the rusty hinges squeal in protest. *So much for a quiet entrance.*

I hear arguing coming from the common room as I pad over, and the creaky floorboards have Spike and Freddy turning towards me. "I'm here. Now, let them all go."

Spike emits a wild sound and closes the gap between us. "Did you really expect to come barging in here, barking orders at me, with no consequences?"

"Wasn't that the deal? If I came, you would let the others go."

"You've changed, Little Wolf." He doesn't seem the least bit surprised by my drastic change in appearance. But I don't have the time or energy to explore that peculiarity any further at the moment.

"I've learned there are people worth fighting for," I counter.

"So, you've finally figured out that it's not all about *you,* huh?"

"Boss, we have some unexpected company!" Freddy blares before running towards the commotion downstairs.

Spike slams me against the wall. "You brought them here?" Ceramic shatters over his head, and he collapses at my feet. I fall to my hands and knees sucking in air.

"Shit, Maya. Are you okay? Did he hurt you?"

I run a hand over my hero's face. "I'm okay, now that you're here, Sable."

He touches his lips to my palm. "Good, because I need to get you out of here *fast.*"

"Wait! What about the prisoners?"

"Do you know where they are?"

I fumble towards the hidden metal door in the corner of the loft. I wrench it open and see three huddled females. "It's safe. You can trust us. Please, we need to hurry." I help them stand before guiding them along the fire escape to the ground floor. "We have to shift if we want to make it back before they come after us." I turn to Sable as he releases Sky from a hug. "Sable, come on. We have to go."

"I can't go with you. I need to help the pack buy you more time. I'll meet you at home." He turns to leave, but I snatch his wrist before kissing him deeply.

"You better come back to me."

He runs his thumbs over my wet cheeks. "Go, please. Or all of this was for nothing."

I glance at the terrified women and nod. They need assistance. More than Sable does. I walk away, forcing myself to not look back. I hear him climb the fire escape, and I pray he keeps his word. "Is everybody ready?" I question the small group.

Sky embraces me. "I can't believe you sacrificed yourself for us, for people you don't even know."

"Isn't that what an alpha does?" I smirk at her. "It's in my blood."

"Sable texted me the moment he found out you were his long-lost mate. He loves you so much. Welcome to the family."

We morph into fur and bullet through the forest until we reach our border. I stop short as the others pad back to the safety of their loved ones. Their cries of joy clench my heart.

I know what I must do now, and I pray I'm not too late.

Sable

Fight for Love

As her shadow is swallowed by darkness, I glare at the staircase leading to Spike's loft. That piece of shit! He should know better than to take what doesn't fucking belong to him. Somebody needs to teach him a lesson. My claws tingle in anticipation, while my wolf practically drools for the metallic taste of his life force.

I'm a little rusty with my fighting skills, considering the last brawl I was in was in fifth grade over Jimmy calling me a doodie-head. But I am a shifter, a born killer! And he fucked up when he took my mate. Out of respect for her wishes, I let it go, hoping he would stay the hell away from us. Then he abducted my baby sister...

The dingy stairs wobble as I take two at a time, ready for blood. When I enter, voices waft from the bedroom. "You have become insignificant," a male roars.

"You would be nothing without me!" Spike growls. "I can still meet the deadline, just follow through with what you promised me in return."

"My men will do their job, mutt. As long as you do yours."

I step into the room just in time to see the loft door close on the stranger. But he isn't the one I came for. My gaze never falters as I circle the sick bastard.

"Have you come back to finish what you started?" Spike cackles. "Or maybe you've come to get some tips on how to make her moan."

I narrow my eyes as a growl erupts. "You'll never put your fucking hands on her again!"

"She won't be happy with you, you know? But, hey, I could always leash you and let you watch me fuck her?"

I charge, colliding with him and taking out a bookshelf. Fists fly wildly. I curse. This man must be on steroids! How the hell can he be matching me punch for punch?

"You're sweating, Sable," he taunts. "Am I exhausting you?" I grunt as he lands an iron fist to my stomach. "You are fucking pathetic!" He spits in my face. "She is a *queen,* who deserves a powerful king, not a weakling."

I slam my elbow into his nose. He falters and I charge him again. We roll over broken furniture, each trying to get the upper hand. Suddenly, I hesitate as I hear gunshots coming from downstairs. What is going on? I panic, thinking about Dad and the rest of the pack battling down there. This isn't how these things work between shifters. We play by the rules, fists and fangs only. Who brought the metal?

Blood drips from Spike's toothy grin. "I have friends in high places, and they've loaned me some new toys."

Of course, El Douche would break the laws to prevail. I need to finish *him*, so I can help *them*. I grab his neck and squeeze. His pulse throbs under my palm. "Any final words?"

His eyes roll back before he crumbles to the floor. As much as I want to end him here and now, the pack needs me. My boots pound down the stairs to the ground floor, and as my feet hit the final step, I jump into action. My eyes scan the horror as it unfolds.

"Sable!"

I pivot to see Aspen pinned with a barrel pointed at his forehead. My skin tingles as my fur expands. The man turns, just in time to go wide-eyed, before I tear his head off and spit it at my brother's feet. Then I clutch Aspen's pants and drag him outside, away from the chaos. "What the fuck are you doing here!" I roar once I'm on two feet again.

"I couldn't just sit at home while everybody fought! When I pulled up, I saw you run upstairs so I followed. But then that man came out of nowhere. I didn't even have time to shift."

"You shouldn't be here!"

"Fuck you!" His words hit hard, and I stumble. "Everybody is always treating me like a little kid! But I'm eighteen!"

"Aspen…"

"No! Stop! I see that look in your eyes! I deserve a chance to protect my family just as much as you do!"

"I was only going to say your fly is down."

"Really? You're going to joke right now?"

I point to his pants with a raised eyebrow, and sure enough, he notices the open pouch. "You want to be treated like a fucking grown man? Start acting like one. Go home. Now."

"But…"

"No!" I roar, slamming him against the building. "I won't watch you get hurt next! Don't you see? That's exactly what Spike wants. First Maya, then Sky, and now you come waltzing in!"

"Fine! Let him try!"

The heat radiating off us is vibrating through the air. Why my

131

little brother decided to grow a pair now is beyond me. But I won't back down. He is too young to make these life-or-death decisions. I'm going to protect him for as long as I can. Aspen's phone rings, and we both blink out of our heated argument before he frowns at the caller ID with Sky's name flashing across it. He quickly answers and pales as his eyes meet mine.

Maya is coming back for me. I cringe as more gunfire sounds in the distance. Shit's about to get real. "You need to stop her, Aspen. Take the woods and force her to turn around. And you both get your asses home!" I don't wait for him to respond before I rush back into the battle.

I should have killed Spike, instead of leaving him passed out on the floor. If Maya sneaks back in and he sinks his claws into her, I'll never forgive myself. I kick his body, watching his chest rise and fall as I clench my fists. I hate having to do this…

I glance around the room. Maybe there are handcuffs or some rope lying around? I could keep him somewhere until the police arrive. As I pivot to take a look, I'm hit from behind and stars twinkle over my vision.

Scarlett

An End

My tongue hangs out and my legs quake as I stride up to the Warehouse. Attempting to locate my family, I sniff. But their scent is all over the place. I shift to two feet and sneak past the battle scene. Bodies litter the ground, some motionless while others in heated hand-to-hand combat. I falter over the slick blood as it pools, and I shiver as my feet splash in the warm substance.

I hear voices coming from the loft, and I climb the stairs two at a time. The door is already thrown off its hinges, and when I turn the corner, I suck in air at the sight. Spike has his massive hands wrapped around Sable's neck. "Stop!"

Spike's bloodshot eyes shoot towards me while crimson oozes from a gash on his head. He has officially lost his sanity. And I'm his next target. He drops my mate in a heap of blood and limbs. "Are you happy now?" he roars. "Did you see what you have caused? All those lost lives! Your friends, my friends, *our* family!"

My legs are cement. I can't break my gaze as it's glued to Sable's form. When his chest doesn't rise, my knees give out and I fall to the floor. My head is too heavy and droops into my shaking hands. "I didn't want this. I came by myself so nobody would get hurt."

"Well, you failed!" Spike tugs me by my hair. "I gave you everything, and *this* is how you repay me!"

"Where's my dad? What did you do?"

"*Your* dad? Your *dad*!" His roar bounces off the walls. "When the fuck did *that* happen? I've been more of a father figure than that murderer! He got what he deserved! What was *owed* to him after he killed my brother! Didn't you see his body amongst the carnage you created?"

I shake my head as tears fall. "No… I finally found them, and you took them away."

I'm too numb to fight him as he tosses me on the bed like a rag doll. "Shh. This is the only place you belong, Scarlett." He nuzzles my neck and breathes in my fragrance. "*My* Little Wolf." His lips caress my neck as he pushes his body on top of mine. "That night I attacked, I swore I wouldn't let you live, that I would avenge my brother's death with your blood." His hand glides between my thighs. "But when you looked into my eyes, I couldn't. That innocence. That beauty."

Sable groans from the floor as he stirs. And hope jolts my heart into beating again. Spike pauses his caress. "Sable, I'm glad I didn't kill you yet. Now you can watch as I devour my queen."

"Let her go," Sable pushes out with effort while attempting to stand, but he falls with a thud.

Spike strokes my cheek. "What do you think? Should I let him watch us? Maybe he could learn a thing or two?" My brain goes into overdrive as he rubs his erection against my clit and flicks his tongue along my breast. Sally starts to push me aside so we can survive another forced entry. "Make sure you scream loud and clear. Remind him who you really belong to," Spike demands as he slips in a finger. "You are wet for me. Yeah, that's right. Let me take care of you, Scarlett."

My eyes shoot open as his implication registers. I won't be his victim *any* longer. I know who I am. And I'm worth *more* than this. I use all my energy and slam my knee into his groin. I'm rewarded with a groan as he falls off the bed. "My name is Maya!" I hiss before sliding farther away, jumping down, and running to Sable to help him stand. "Are you okay?"

"I told you to return home."

"If you're going to be my mate, you are going to have to get used to my rule-breaking." Before he can respond, a gun cocks behind us.

Spike aims the barrel at me. "If I can't have you, then nobody will." Sable growls, shifting and leaping as his fangs clamp down on Spike's neck before he shakes his head wildly. Blood splatters the walls. Spike howls in pain as they both fall to the floor. The once-terrifying pack leader gasps for air as he meets my eyes. "I only wanted the best for you…" He gurgles, then his head falls to the side.

I run my hand over his face, closing his eyes. "I hope you find peace."

Sable tugs me to him. "Are you hurt?"

"No." I turn my head at the sound of police cars approaching, their lights dancing on the walls. This is going to take a lot of explaining.

Sable never releases my hand, even after we are checked out of the hospital and have talked with the cops. I'm surprised by how much the police department actually knows about shifters. They even have their own task force for these *sensitive* situations, and the two investigators assigned to us are both shifters from another pack.

By the time we make it back to our territory, it is well into the early morning hours. I choke on a sob when I see my mom and dad in the archway of our cave. We embrace and my mom strokes my hair. "We would have met you at the hospital, but we were trying to settle everybody here and we knew you were in good hands."

Sable pulls on my wrist. "Maya, I should check on Sky and make sure my family is safe."

But after this long day, and almost losing him, I can't let him leave. "Sable, I want to check on your family too, if that's okay?"

"You're always welcome at our home."

My dad steps forward. "I don't like this. We have more pack members here, for *your* protection."

"But the one person who was after me is dead." I frown at his stern expression. "Look, I appreciate everything you've done for me. *But* I wasn't asking your permission. I *need* this. Please try to understand."

My dad purses his lips, but Mom grabs his wrist and shakes her head. "I will try to respect your wishes, for now. Here, take this with you, in case you need us," my dad grinds out.

"You're giving me a cell phone?"

"Well, it sure beats howling."

I know this is hard for my parents. They just got me back, and

I'm running straight into Sable's arms. *And* spending time with *his* family.

"You can call, text, or howl all you want. I'll always answer back," I respond.

My dad tosses Sable a set of keys. "You're both exhausted, so skip the shift and take my car. But not a scratch on it. Now go, before I come to my senses and take it all back."

I am bone-tired, even walking to my dad's car is a feat. Once we are on the road, I settle into the leather seat and rest my eyes. "You weren't supposed to come back," Sable whispers.

"You're welcome, you know, for saving your ass."

"If you would have just stayed—"

"Then you would be dead, and my life would be meaningless again!" I shout, causing a tense silence.

Sable parks the car in front of his house and pivots towards me. "I had to lie there and watch him touch you. Do you have any idea how *infuriating* that was? To watch the woman I love, being molested? I was helpless."

"So was I. For almost a year, I have been at his mercy. Forced to my knees for his sick pleasure, because of his personal vendetta against my father. I needed to confront him, Sable. I had to get my closure." I squeeze his fingertips. "So I can move on to my happily ever after."

He brings my hand to his lips. "You are my world, Maya."

As soon as we get out of the car, I embrace Sable. My mind won't stop replaying all the violence we endured. And even after our last conversation, I need more reassurance. "In your arms, I am safe, whole, and loved. Promise me you will never let me go."

Sable kisses the top of my head. "You'll never get rid of me. I'm yours always and forever." He places a finger under my chin and lifts my lips to his. And I melt into his arms. When I breathe in his scent, I tense. *I can't believe it!*

Sable

Untrustworthy

Maya shoves off me before she marches into the house with a look that could kill. What the fuck did I do? I replay everything. It was going so well. "What's wrong?" I shout at her.

Once she is inside, I hear a crash and screams, so I race into the living room. The scene has fur pushing past my skin. Maya is on top of the Fangs' beta. That son of a bitch! But as I step forward to rip his head off his shoulders, my sister interjects, waving her hands in the air wildly. "Get off him!" Sky shouts as she tugs on Maya.

"Yes, get off him, so I can tear him from limb to limb!" I roar.

The prick glances from me to Maya and decides to reason with the clearer-headed one. "Listen, it wasn't what it looked like, okay? Sky came with me *willingly*."

"Bullshit! My sister would never trust a dirtbag like you! Especially after tonight!"

"He's telling the truth." Sky shoves Maya to the side and stands over Freddy protectively. "Back off and stop being a hypocrite! You're trying to marry Spike's bed buddy, and no one's batting a lash. Why can't you hear Freddy out, like you did for her?"

Maya side-steps the pair and clutches her chest. I glare at Sky for causing that agony. She has no idea what Maya went through with that douchebag. And to compare my mate to this piece of garbage is inexcusable!

But my sister is headstrong and used to getting what she wants. I need *her* to see what an asshole Freddy is, so she leaves him of her own volition and not because I demand it. "Explain yourself then! Before I decide my sister has lost her damn mind and kill you without even shifting."

"Everybody, please sit down and take a deep breath. Freddy was just finishing up telling us what happened." Dad's eyes land on each of ours. His alpha tone laces each word.

We slowly lower onto the sofa, ready to pounce at a moment's notice. I collect the wounded Maya in my lap and nuzzle her neck, trying to pull her out of her despair.

"Freddy and I have been dating for three months now," Sky starts.

"What the hell! He is just tricking you, using you to get information."

"Freddy is *nothing* like Spike." Sky glares. "He warned me what was going on before it even happened."

"Then why didn't you tell *us*? We would have protected you."

"Because everything happened so fast, Sable. We had to make it look real, or Spike would have suspected us and we both would have been killed."

My sister is helping the enemy now? I rub a hand over my stubble. This is too much. And why didn't Carly warn me about this? She and Sky are closer than sisters—if sisters fooled around in college, that is. Something doesn't add up.

"Listen, you don't have to believe us. But it's true." Sky squeezes Freddy's hand. "I love him and nothing you say will change my mind." She stands while she guides Freddy to her room without a backwards glance.

"Sky!" I boom, trying to recover from her betrayal. "We aren't done talking about this!" I turn my scowl on my dad. "Innocent men died so that we could set her free, and she is sleeping with their murderer? And you are allowing this scumbag into our home?" My accusation rings out, challenging the alpha.

"In time, I hope Freddy and Sky will give you the whole story, son. But from what they explained, I feel confident that everybody is safe."

My family has finally lost their minds. Am I the only sane one left? My perusal of the room confirms it. Should I fight them on this? One glance at my defeated mate is answer enough. If my family wants to misplace their trust, fine. But I'm sure as hell protecting what is mine! "Just make certain to call Frost and explain it to him—explain how you're not taking the trash out and allowing his only child to stay here with him in the next room."

At the mention of my adult sleepover, Mom's eyes dance with mischief. "It's a blessing to have such a full home. Thank you for helping us fill it, dear Maya."

Poor Maya takes my mother in stride as she nods and blushes profusely. I grin as I wonder what my mate is thinking, because there is only one thing I've had on *my* mind. And that's reclaiming what's always been *mine*. I'll devour every inch of her body while reminding her how fucking remarkable she is. I'll ravish her until there is no doubt in her head.

I swear, if it's the last thing I do, I'll ease her misery. She'll never again question where she belongs, or who she is.

Scarlett

Mates

Sable leads me to his room, tugging faster as we pass Sky's. "I can't believe Dad is letting him sleep across the hall from us." He slams his door and locks it.

Before he can complain further, I press my lips against him and wrap my arms around his neck. "Thank you for saving my life, Sable."

"Thank you for saving mine."

We lean our foreheads together and breathe in each other's scents. The world is perfect whenever we are like this. Nobody can separate us. Nothing can come between us. Except…

Oh no. What if mates are supposed to save themselves for one another? Have I damned our relationship? "I'm so sorry, Sable."

"What do you have to be sorry about?"

"I don't have anything to offer you. I gave my virginity to Spike."

I see rage cross his features before he squeezes me. "I don't expect anything from you, only your love and friendship *if* you are willing to give them to me."

"That's all?"

He caresses my cheek and cups my chin. He lowers his lips to mine, but before they touch, he whispers, "Will you love me and be my best friend?"

"You accept me, as is? Bruised and broken, with literally nothing to offer you in return?"

"Always and forever."

My lips quiver before I kiss him deeply. He returns my intensity with his own, and our bodies burn with desire. I reach for his hard member, but Sable pulls away slowly.

"I'm in desperate need of a shower."

"Oh, I understand." I turn to leave but he pulls me to his chest.

"If you want, we could conserve water and shower together?"

"I've never done that before," I whisper.

"Me either." His eyes sparkle as he grins down at me. "It'll be our first shower with another person. Our first *first*."

"Yes, I'd like that."

He turns on the water and clears his throat as his eyes eat up my frame.

"Sable, are you nervous?" I try to hide my smirk. It's cute. Even with all this alpha nonsense, I can tell he isn't in his comfort zone.

"No, of course not. I just want to make sure *you* are comfortable. I won't force you to do anything you don't want to do."

My body warms as my hand runs over his chest. He leans in to my touch with a soft groan. Then I reach for his dick but pause as images of Spike's abuse invade my mind. "No." I rub furiously at my eyes, demanding they stop.

"Maya?" He tries to hold me, but I push him off.

"I'm sorry. I thought I could. But I'm hopeless."

"Hey, don't say that." He gently grabs my hand and squeezes until I meet his tender gaze. "We will move as slow as you need. I'm in no rush." He kisses my palm. "Do you want to jump in the shower first?"

I shake my head before nudging him forward. He climbs in and I watch his dark silhouette against the shower curtain.

What's wrong with you? I chastise myself. *Sable is not Spike. They are completely different.*

The sight of my mate's hands roving over his body makes my mouth water. Oh, wow. This is the best porn ever. When he reaches to lather his private area, my thighs clasp together as warmth settles there. *Oh. Dear.* I need to do something. *Think!* "Sable, can I wash your back?" I blurt out. *Really! That's your plan? To join the sausage fest.*

Without hesitation, he passes me the sudsy luffa. His eyes darken and beg me to worship him, before he pivots and puts his palms flat on the tiled wall. He rests his forehead between his hands, giving me full view of his backside. I nibble my bottom lip, as I slide the soap across his spine. Once he is covered in white suds, I set the soap down and run my nails over his muscles. A shiver racks his body before he leans in to my touch. As my hands near his rear, I squeeze his tight glutes beneath my fingertips. So many delicious images cloud my mind.

"I thought you wanted to wash my *back*."

I jump out of my fantasy and clear my throat. "Sorry, I don't know what I was thinking."

Sable pivots and seizes my hand. "Don't be sorry. I love your touch. Is there anywhere *else* you want to… *wash* for me?"

I force my eyes to look at his face and not *lower*. "Uh, no, thank you."

He smirks while he picks up the soap, his eyes never leaving mine. "I'll take it from here, but if you change your mind, let me know." I envy the suds as his hand rubs them over his member. And just when I think it can't get hotter, he chokes his bulge and tugs it to its full length.

Oh my. I look away from his plaything and meet his lustful gaze. When I lick my lips, his breathing hitches and his speed increases. As he grunts out my name, his eyes close and he releases his load. That was…

Intense.

When the water shuts off, I squeak and scurry to the other side of the bathroom with my back to him, so he has plenty of room to get out and get dressed. *And* to hide my embarrassment.

I'm such a perve.

I straighten when hot steam tickles my back. Is he standing behind me? Then his lips dance along my neck in a featherlight touch while his fingertips glide over my arms. "Can I watch you get wet?" Warmth spreads to my toes at his husky, needy tone. He takes my hesitation as an answer and kisses my cheek. "I didn't mean to make you uncomfortable. I'll change in the room and give you some privacy."

My body screams with the loss of heat. "Wait." My shaking limbs collect the hem of my shirt before I pull it off and toss it aside. I slip out of my jeans and stand there, self-conscious and uncertain. My arms coil around my midsection and I look away. What was I thinking?

In two quick strides, Sable pushes me against the wall and kisses me deeply. "You are so beautiful. I'm the luckiest man alive." His lips touch every part of my exposed skin, and soon, I relax and allow my head to fall back so I can enjoy his gentle exploration. He is nothing like Spike. Sable is so patient and kind. He pulls away and starts the shower. "I'll see you in the room." He kisses the top of my head before he shuts the door.

My fingers glide over the areas Sable kissed and I shiver. Is this how it's supposed to feel? Being with a man who respects you?

As the soap slides over my body, I pretend it's his hand, and I moan. I could get used to his soft caresses. I quickly rinse, then pat myself dry with a towel. My hand lingers on the bathroom doorknob, and I take a deep breath. *I want him.* When I open the door, I peek over at the bed. Sable glances up from his paperback before setting it aside. I blush as I step towards him. "Sable, I don't know how to do this."

He throws back the covers and opens his arms. I run to him and he wraps them around me. I nuzzle his neck and breathe in. His scent is the strongest aphrodisiac. I flick my tongue over his jawline to get a taste. He arches, granting access to the rest of his collar. I take the invitation and run with it, kissing every inch.

Then he grips my waist and sets me on top of him. "I'm not sure what you have been through. And I hope one day you can confide in me and tell me everything. But if this is what you really want, you need to take charge. I won't do anything unless you ask me to. I don't want to scare you off. You mean too much to me." He falls back against the pillows, watching me as I straddle him.

He will do whatever *I* want? "Kiss me."

He leans forward and obeys. At first, the kiss is slow and sweet. I hold his cheeks and take the lead when I slip my tongue into his mouth and explore. I feel him reach out to touch my body, but he stops midway and clenches his hands. "Please let me touch you." His gentle request is like sweet honey; it beckons me.

"Yes, touch me."

"Where?"

"Everywhere," I whimper as I arch my back. He gently lays me down and runs his hands over my chest. I reach out and trail mine along his arms. The ache in my core is building. "I need you inside me." I position him on top of me and devour his mouth. But when he doesn't proceed, I stare into his eyes. "I understand that you don't want to hurt me. But the only way to heal is to take the next step. Please don't make me beg."

My plea is his undoing. He nuzzles my nipples with his nose, making me throw my head back. Then he licks around my areola but never touches the peaks. The teasing drives me crazy. I grasp a handful of his hair and lead him in the right direction. Finally, he rewards me by taking my breast into his mouth, sending ripples of pleasure throughout my body.

I guide my palm over his tip. He groans but doesn't budge. "Are you sure?" he questions.

"Stop second-guessing all my decisions and make love to me." For a split-second, I'm afraid he's going to deny me, but he teases my core with his tip before entering, his eyes never leaving mine.

The gentle movements drive me nuts, and I take matters into my own hands. I grasp his hips and dig my nails into them. "Faster."

"Let's just take our time. I don't want to cause you any discomfort."

"Stop treating me like a broken mess. Treat me like your mate. I *promise* I will tell you if it's too much for me."

He thrusts in response. Yes, this is much better. Every delicious movement hits just the right spot. It's like our bodies are made for each other, and he knows exactly what to do. *And how.*

The intensity drives me over the edge and I climax, screaming his name into his shoulder as my nails claw his back in pure ecstasy. "That's music to my ears," he mumbles against my lips. Then he pumps until he pours into me. Once our breathing regulates, he scans my face for any sign of regret. "Are you feeling okay?"

"More than okay."

"Okay enough for another go?" He returns my grin before he bends down to claim my mouth, not holding back this time. I shiver as I feel him harden inside me. And as if the bell has been rung, round two begins.

Scarlett

Moving Forward

I start as I hear rustling in the house. I run my fingertips through Sable's hair, before I slip on my clothes and tiptoe out into the hallway. As I near the kitchen, I narrow my eyes, slip my shoe off, and throw it at its intended target.

"Son of a bitch." Freddy rubs the back of his head. "What the hell is your problem?"

"You don't have anybody here to protect you now, you little shit." I flick my wrist, extending my knife. "Come on, for old times' sake."

"Do you really think I'm dumb enough to fall for your bullshit, Scarlett?"

"Call me Scarlett one more time and find out. I won't allow you to ruin this family. They don't see the real you yet, and I don't intend to wait around until they do. Leave, now."

He straightens to his full height. "You should know better than to threaten me. Especially now that Spike isn't around to protect you."

His threat slaps me across my face, and I charge. His eyes pop out before his back slams into the kitchen table. There is a crash, then the wood splinters under our weight, and we flop onto the floor.

"Enough of this! What makes you think I must prove myself to *you*? You bounce from bed to bed to get men wrapped around your finger. You have no right to judge me. I *love* Sky, and we have been dating for months. How long were you dating Spike before you slept with him? Or how about Sable?" He pins my arms and forces me to listen. "We were both compelled to do things we never would've done otherwise, Scar—*Maya*," he corrects. "Don't think you are the only one who deserves a chance to be happy. Or a chance to prove who you really want to be. That you're not the person somebody *forced* you to become. I deserve it too. So, pull your head out of your ass and let me have a damn chance."

Give Freddy a second chance? That's a joke! He was Spike's right-hand man—surely, he knew what his boss was up to. He should have reported it, or stepped up and took over, if he didn't like what was happening. But…

What if Sable never gave me a second chance? A new life? I would still be out in the streets, begging and freezing. "Freddy?"

"Yes, Maya."

"Get your lard ass off me before I kill you."

He chuckles as he rolls to the side and walks to Sky.

"You two were just going to sit there and watch him crush me?"

"Trust me, if Sky wasn't here to stop me, I would have ripped his throat out for touching you." Sable throws a glare at Freddy before tugging on my wrist. "Come with me. I want to show you something."

A grin spreads across his face as he removes his clothing and shifts out the front door. I giggle and follow, itching to feel the wind in my fur again. After the initial clumsy trot, we gallop at full speed for a few miles. My tongue hangs out as I stretch my limbs. At the top of a wide hill, he lifts his nose into the air before he howls from the depths of his throat. Something inside me stirs and I repeat his actions. And we both howl as the sun rises in the distance. I nuzzle his neck while the orange and red hues touch the rest of the world. The sun warms my soul, and for once, I'm optimistic about my future.

"Locals call this place Willow Creek Hill, but to us, it's just Willow Hill." I gaze into the vast area and squint at a cloud of dust. Sable notices my stare and continues to speak through his wolf telepathy. *"The reservation is home to many protected plants and animals, including wild horses."*

"That's amazing!"

"It's not the only thing..."

I smirk at his corny remark, and he continues to stare at me. The silence is welcoming until we hear the padding of eight paws coming our way. We turn to see Sky and Freddy galloping up. They sit and gaze into the distance. Sky rubs her face on Freddy with a look of contentment. I'm going to continue to keep an eye on him. His intentions seem true, but I will never fully trust him.

Sable nips my neck before he bullets into the woods. My tail sways a mile a minute, hitting Sky in the face, and I take off after my mate. We play for hours in the woodlands, until we are both panting and our legs are burning. I lap at the cold liquid from the stream—the same spot where Aspen found me all those nights ago. And I thank my lucky stars Luna put him in my path. I tilt my head and prick my ears as the brush shakes and the roosting birds flee upwards.

I yelp as something tackles me, and we fall in the freezing water. In my confusion, I shift back and glare at Aspen's wolf form. I dunk his head until the bubbles get dangerously low. Then he shifts and coughs in my face. Once we make it to shore, I'm shivering. I snatch Sable's outstretched hand, flop on the cozy grass, and stare into the sky with labored breaths. Sable's warmth pulls me to him before he nuzzles my neck, and I rest my head on his chest. "I love you."

My heart swells at his confession. I lie on top of him, grinning, as my white hair cascades around his. "I love you too. Thank you for this morning. It was perfect."

Aspen passes Sable a small box, then moves away.

"Do you know what would make this more perfect?" Sable massages my hand then places a small object on my finger. I look down and see a beautiful diamond ring. "Maya Tala, will you make me the happiest crazy wolfman alive and marry me?"

I laugh as warm tears sprinkle his chest. Before I met Sable, I was nowhere near ready to settle down. But now, I can't imagine a life without him. Unable to verbalize an answer, I kiss him instead. My head shoots up as I hear thunderous applause. I'm surprised to see our parents have joined us. I bury my red face in Sable's neck.

"There will be plenty of time to celebrate later. But we need to get you ready." My mom helps me up. "Because tonight is our annual gathering."

"Why tonight?"

"It's the night of the Wolf Moon."

"The girls and I put *this* together for you." Sky places a gift bag in my palm.

I unwrap penis-shaped candies, necklaces, bookmarks, and a

ceramic dish advertising that you can *paint your own boyfriend.* "Uh, thanks?"

"If we had more time, we'd have a proper bachelorette party. So, while we get ready, we'll eat, drink, and celebrate your last night as an unclaimed wolf!" Sky links arms with me. As she chatters on about the ceremony, I fiddle with my engagement ring, unable to wipe the grin off my face.

"Tonight, we gather to bring Maya Tala and Sable Canis together as mates. Luna, in all her mighty wisdom, has somehow brought them together through thick and thin. Thank you, Luna, we praise you." Dad sips from the ceremonial wine before he passes the cup to me. I watch Sable as I swallow the red liquid and give it to him. His eyes never leave mine as he repeats my action and hands it to his sister.

The same herb that had made me nervous and unsure with Spike now has me giddy. Once the wine reaches my dad again, we clap and start dancing. Sable twirls me before he holds me close as we sway in the fire light. I'm so happy my cheeks are burning from smiling. "Let me show you something." Sable tugs on my hand.

"You've already shown me plenty," I purr against his chest. We follow a worn trail through the forest, until he stops at a dilapidated tree house. I tilt my head, trying to decipher why he brought me here.

"Do you remember this place?" I arch a brow in response but decide to humor him. I trail my fingertips over the leaves while I observe my surroundings. A red twig catches my eye, and I pull it down. To my surprise, it's not a branch at all, but an old doll. Sable collects the moldy thing and sighs. "Old Red has seen better days."

"Red?"

He hands me the plush. "She was the reason you ran off that night."

"What do you mean?" I brush off the moss that covers her eyes.

"Your mom said they were cooking and settling down for the night, but you insisted on grabbing Red so you could play with her. Then you took off, right into the dark woods, not a care in the world. Your uncle caught up with you, and, well..." His voice drops.

My dream! The man I trusted, the one who died... "It's all my fault."

"You were only three years old. And if we had thought there was trouble in our haven, we never would have let you go out. But after all those years had passed without an incident, we assumed Spike was over his brother's loss. Who knew he was just sitting and waiting for the right moment to strike?" Sable bumps my shoulder with his. "Did you know I had a matching doll?"

"You liked to play with girl toys?"

"Hey, it was a boy doll! His name was Andy." He collects my hand and tugs me away from the haunting structure. "When we have kids, I'll clean this place up and make it habitable again."

"I would love that, Mr. Handyman. Why didn't you tell me you owned your own car shop?"

"It's a mechanic's shop," he corrects.

"Hey, I know absolutely nothing about cars, tools, or even shopping. *So*, excuse me."

"Oh, yet another thing I get to teach you?"

"Am I wearing you down, old man?"

"I'm only six years older than you."

"Yikes, I may need to find a younger mate."

He tosses me over his shoulder and smacks my ass. "You better watch it, or you won't be able to sit for a week."

"Promises, promises."

His chuckle bounces off the trees before the forest opens up to a clearing. "Let me show you how to build a *real* fire."

"Hey! I know my way around a fire!"

"Yes, I remember that dinky little thing you built in that cave."

That feels so long ago now... I grin, recalling the day we met. "I'd love the opportunity to start a real *inferno*, if you're up for the heat?" I grab a fistful of his butt and squeeze.

"Is that so?" He sets me back on the ground and devours my mouth, taking my breath away. When he pulls back, he rubs my swollen lips. "How's that?"

"I think I can do better." I giggle as he dips me and caresses my neck. I toss my clothes into the grass, shift, and dash into the woods. Sable tugs my tail before taking the lead. I quickly recover and match his stride until we reach Willow Hill. We rest and witness the full moon complete its ascent. I could sit here and watch the animals scamper all day. I make a mental note to check out the caverns below, where Dad said there are paintings from earlier settlers. I pivot to invite Sable on a moonlit stroll, but when our eyes meet, desire flickers back at me. He rubs his fur muzzle over my body, and I close my lids.

My wolf instincts take over and my tail eagerly lifts, begging him to satiate my animalistic needs. My body quivers in anticipation as he strides behind me. Once he reaches his desired location, he runs his tongue over my opening, tasting my readiness. When I don't protest, he mounts and nips my scruff. His movements are slow at first while he lets me adjust to his size and position. The action causes my mind to spiral. It's not long before I'm whimpering my release, and he follows suit. We shift back and snuggle beneath the dying moonlight.

"Are you happy?"

I run my hand through his hair. "I'm the happiest I have ever been." The ceremonial wine wears off, but it doesn't hinder my natural high as I lie in the arms of the man who loves me. When we return to the pack, breakfast is already laid out. We settle between my parents and the beta, taking on our new roles as alphas in training.

It feels weird to climb the hierarchy so fast, but Dad ensures me that it's always been my birthright, that it's in my *blood* to lead. I side-glance the beta, Jackson, as he ruffles a pup's head when the kid snatches a rib off his plate before a chase ensues. Technically, he *was* next in line, without me in the picture, but he hasn't shown any contempt towards me. I smirk as I catch my mate's eyes. Sable, on the other hand, Jackson doesn't seem to care for. But from what's been explained to me, it has something to do with the past and nothing to do with the current chain of command.

"Maya, we got you something," Mom announces.

"Thank you, but you didn't need to get me anything."

"Of course we did, sweetie. You didn't think we would forget your birthday, did you?"

My mom's words echo in my head. Since I was dropped off without any information, I never figured out what day it actually fell on. "The exact date has always been a mystery; no one could tell me when I was born." My mom blinks as the realization hits her. She embraces me, and I pat her back, unsure how to comfort her waterfall of emotions.

"Well, the important thing is you know now. And we have sixteen birthday parties to cram into one. Right, Raven?" Sable concludes, rushing to my aid.

"That's a great idea. I'm going to make the *biggest* party ever for my baby girl." Mom strides towards her cave, wiping at her eyes. I massage the back of my neck as I stare down at her neglected gift. I peel off the wrapping paper.

"Well, I guess the next thing on my to-do list will be to get a driver's license." I jiggle the key at Sable.

"Oh, you never learned to drive?"

"If I didn't even know my birthday, how do you propose I get a driver's license?" I retort.

"I'm sorry. I didn't mean it like that."

"It's not your fault." I rub his hand. "It's just overwhelming. I never realized how much I didn't even know about myself."

"Well, then it's a wonderful thing you are now married to an amazing mechanic, who is also a terrific driver. Don't worry, we will figure everything out *together*."

"I'm so glad you are in my life. You keep me *sane*."

"That's good to hear, because you are going to need all that sanity soon enough. Trust me… your mother will go above and beyond for your celebration. Just you wait and see."

I groan, but secretly I can't wait.

Scarlett

First Hunt

I stare into the valley at a loss for words. My mother did it. She constructed sixteen birthday parties all into one big celebration complete with a bounce house, a Slip 'N Slide, volleyball, horseshoes, pony rides, and every food imaginable. "Mom, you didn't have to go through all this trouble for me."

"Nonsense! It's the least I could do." She kisses my head. "And by this time next year, you will be a licensed driver. I'm so proud of you."

"Now, wait just a minute. Before she gets her driver's license, she needs to complete a hunt."

"Dad, I don't think I'm ready for *that*."

"We have been training for this. Don't worry about it. You have my blood in your veins, and your wolf's instincts will kick in when the time comes."

"Oh, stop pushing the girl, Frost." Granny elbows her way through.

"I'm so glad you could make it, Ma." Dad pulls a chair out for her.

"I wouldn't miss my grandbaby's birthday parties. Now, let me have a look at you. You are absolutely glowing, Maya. Here, have this." She slides a package towards me.

"Thank you." I rip the paper off and smile at a silver necklace. "It's beautiful."

"I bought it for you… for your fourth birthday." She swipes at her eye. "But better late than never." I clasp it on before running my hand over the wolf pendant. "Now, leave this old lady to her punch and go enjoy yourselves." She taps her cane against my shoe. "Especially that sweet potato."

Sable grasps my hands. "I want to see you ride a pony."

"Oh, I bet you do. Anything else you want to watch me ride?" I wink at his carefree smile. I feel like a little kid who just woke up to the best Christmas ever.

The next morning, I rub my eyes, staring into the sunless sky. "When I agreed to this, I didn't think it would be the day after my party." I yawn. "And does the hunt have to be so early? My cheeks are still numb from sleep." I yelp as Sable grabs my butt before collecting me in his arms and kissing my face.

"Will you two cut it out!" Jackson glares. "You're scaring off the prey."

"Oh, stop it. We are not. You're just jealous," I grumble.

"And you are a whiney brat. Stop complaining. We all go on our first hunt when we turn ten years old."

"Well, since I was kidnapped by a fucking psycho, I couldn't."

"I come with peace offerings of coffee and donuts," Aspen announces, throwing his hand over his mouth to cover a yawn.

"Thank you," Sable interjects, trying to break up my feud with the beta. The tension is thicker than the morning fog. We all tilt back our paper cups waiting for my dad's signal.

"Maya, I'm sorry I called you a whiney brat," Jackson mumbles over his lid.

"And I'm sorry I called you a jackass."

He stops mid-sip and arches his brow. "Wait, when did you call me that?"

"Just now." I stick my tongue out. But before he can respond, there's a loud bird call.

"All right, there's the signal. Finish those coffees and stretch those limbs. It's going to be a long morning."

We shift and move lightning fast down the tree line. The cool breeze combs my fur while my paws pound the earth. Suddenly, my snout catches a mouthwatering scent, then my eyes land on the herd of deer. My muscles ripple as I bound towards my target. The creatures raise their heads in unison before locking on to our pack and scampering away. The thought of chasing them makes my body tingle with anticipation. We quicken our strides and mercilessly fly across the wooded area. I spring forward, claws extended, until I slam on top of my kill and sink my fangs into the soft flesh of its neck. My wolf relishes the crimson liquid as it spurts at my paws.

"That was a good attack," Dad praises when he shifts to his human form. As he passes, he scratches behind my ear, causing my foot to bounce and my tongue to loll out.

"I would have had it, if she didn't cut me off at the bend." Sable pouts as he helps Dad collect the corpse.

I stand on two feet and throw him a grin. "Don't be jealous that I got a kill on my first try."

Jackson pats me on the back. "You should have seen your husband on *his* first hunt. How many times did it take you?" Sable flips him off. "On his first attempt, the poor guy landed in a pond and got soaking wet. When he tried again, the deer swerved so fast Sable didn't have time to detour and ran headfirst into a poison ivy bush."

I can't suppress my laughter as I imagine the chaos. I'm glad Sable isn't this hotshot, perfect man. "You can laugh all you want. But now you have to skin and cut the carcass." Sable smirks.

"Do I have to? I did most of the work to catch it."

"Maya, it's important to know how to do this bit too," Dad throws over his shoulder.

Once we are out of the woods, I lift my hands to the clear blue sky to soak in the sun's welcoming rays. It's great doing something for my fellow pack members. This deer will feed all of us, and nothing will go to waste. Even if I have to get my hands dirty, I'm finally contributing.

I glance up at Jackson. Even that jackass is growing on me.

Sable

Back to Business

"I'm going to miss you," Maya purrs against my chest.

I knead her ass, and she rewards me by thrusting her hips into mine. "I promise, *tonight,* I'm all yours," I whisper in her ear. "So, add *that* to your to-do list, and I'll make your dreams come true."

"All of them? Even if I want to double up?" She grins against my cheek.

"Wait… double up on what, exactly?"

Her laughter is everything to me. "Dates—a double date."

She must be talking about my sister and Freddy. Although Freddy says he's innocent when it comes to most of his alleged transgressions, there is *no* way I want to break bread with that asshat. "How about I double up on your orgasms instead?"

A male clears his throat from behind us. Dumbass Jackson—I could strangle him. Frost says his presence is required for Maya's training and protection, but I call bullshit.

"I should go." She kisses me softly. "Have a good day at work."

"I'm counting down the seconds until I can have you underneath me."

Her blush is worth every word, even as she pushes me towards the auto shop entrance. I pivot, collect her in my arms, and claim her mouth. When I pull away, she is breathless and runs her hand down my face. "I love you."

"I love you more." I watch her hips as she sways towards the woods. I readjust myself before I enter the shop. As I pass the front desk, I wave to Aspen, then head towards the bays in the back.

"Well, look who finally graced us with his presence." Chuck smirks. "And here I thought you were too good for us, now that you're married and training to be king of the jungle. I even believed you might *finally* sign the shop over to me."

"In your fucking dreams," I grumble. "Now, why don't you exercise your more *important* muscles and get to work on that damn Mazda… the one that should have been finished last week?"

"Mark my words, brother: once you need diaper money, you'll be ready to sell."

I roll my eyes as I hide under the Durango's hood. I won't counter with the fact that my family is very well off. We want for nothing. Maya and our children can have whatever they desire, and then some. That's one plus side to being a shifter. We hunt and farm for most of our food and work hard to pay for anything else. Chuck has been on my ass to sell him half the shop, but that man is a gambler, and I don't need him using the business as collateral. That's how he lost his Harley a few years ago. He's an excellent mechanic but a horrible businessman.

I twist my wrist and the ratchet clicks into place. It feels good to be tinkering again. Although, if Frost had his way, I'd be out training in the woods with him and Maya. Thank Luna my parents stood up to the insufferable alpha and reminded him of my thriving shop. But I'm not sure how long that is going to hold him off. He is dedicated to making my life a living hell. Even if he is labeling it as *alpha training*, he knows damn well that I'm more than proficient when it comes to hunting and building a campfire.

Don't get me wrong, I love spending time with Maya. And I'll gladly spend every waking second with her by my side, but I need to have my own thing too. And this grease hole is it. Especially when she decides she doesn't want this stupid alpha position. It's more of a hassle than anything else. But I'm not going to force my beliefs on her. I want her to make her own mind up. I mean, once Frost's grumpy ass dies, I might consider selling the shop. But right now, I can't be in constant close quarters with him: dealing with him breathing down my back, telling me *everything* I'm doing wrong, and reminding me (as often as he can) that Maya is *his* daughter.

Then there's the Tala pack's second in command, Jackson. He's been training to be beta for years and his lips are permanently sewn to Frost's ass, doing exactly what the man says and when. He hasn't said anything out loud, but I can tell he isn't happy with Maya's return. Because that knocks him out of the running to become the next alpha.

Before all of this, it was easy to be a silent member of the pack, because I'd return to my home and call it a day. But I need to keep the peace between everyone, especially now that I'm living inside the territory.

The things I do for my mate. I can't help the grin that spreads at the thought of her. She is everything I hoped for and more.

"Sable, Frost is on the phone for you. He said it's urgent."

"Aspen, just take a message." Once my brother returns to the office, my cell phone rings in my pocket. "Son of a fur-fuck." I slam my finger on the screen. "What do you want??"

"We have a situation."

"What else is new?" I grind out. "I'm working right now. I'll report back to you when I get home, then we can discuss whatever this is."

"Can you pull your head out of your ass for one damn minute!" he roars. "We have a situation, and I *need* your help."

My ratchet stills. "Sorry, service *must* be going out. What did you say?"

"Stop fucking around. I need you here with the pack. You are our future alpha, and this is important."

"What's up, Frost?"

"*He* is here."

My blood runs cold. "Why?"

"He's blaming Maya for the attack on the Warehouse and looking to reprimand her."

"Over my dead body!" I stomp towards the exit, eager to beat the shit out of anyone threatening my woman.

"We have to put our past behind us, Sable, and fight together—on a *united* front—if we are going to save her."

I swallow down all the misdeeds of the past, exchanging them for a more pleasant future. "I agree. See you soon."

Scarlett

Guardian

It took a while, but I finally convinced my dad that it's safe to explain the wolf stuff to Sara. I mean, her adoptive parents descend from the tribe that has protected our pack for generations, so odds are she already knows or *will* eventually. After spewing all the facts, I wait for a response. As she processes, I watch as two butterflies dance around a bright yellow flower. I breathe in the warmer air, glad winter's edge is melting and that spring is pushing through.

"I can't believe you got married and didn't even invite me." Sara pouts. Really? Out of everything, *that's* what she cares about? "And you *look* totally different." She kicks my foot. "Why is everything changing so fast with you?"

"I already explained it to you. You don't believe me?"

"Would *you* believe it if someone told you they could turn into a dog?"

"It's a wolf, not a dog."

"They are in the same family."

I pull the small girl into an embrace as the sun warms our skin. "I missed you too, Sara. Enough about me. How do you like your new family?"

"They are nice, and it feels good having three meals a day, my own room, and new clothes. But it's hard to remember to follow the rules. I get in trouble a lot… I'm afraid they will decide they don't want me anymore and return me."

"I talked to Debbie, and she said she *loves* your free spirit. She even mentioned how you are thriving in school and always willing to help her around the house with chores and cooking." I elbow her. "I didn't know you knew how to cook or clean."

"Maya, is that one of your family members?"

I follow her gaze until I spot my mom in wolf form at the edge of the woods. She stands there observing from a distance, her amber eyes unwavering. I jolt as the porch door closes behind us. "I'm sorry to cut your visit short but, Sara, sweetheart, it's time for you to get going on your homework."

"That's one of the rules I was talking about," Sara grumbles before skipping inside. Debbie rubs her arms, plagued by an invisible chill. "Be careful, Maya, my skin is crawling with uncertainty."

Dad explained Debbie's family history and hinted that she's acquainted with the magic of her people. So I heed her advice. "Thank you. I will keep my eyes open for trouble. Have a good night."

I pat my mom's head and cross into our territory with her trailing behind. Then it hits me as I sniff the landscape: there's a stranger in our midst. Mom gallops past me, and her tail fades into the distance. I slip my dress over my head. Why haven't wolves learned to shift without shredding their clothing? I hold the fabric in my teeth before I turn skin to fur. I easily pass my mom and nip at her rear as I go. She retaliates, snapping at my tail but I tuck it under my body, lower my head, and take off like a bullet in the wind.

My dad waits at the entrance of our territory. I skid to a halt, throwing loose dirt into the air. I rub my head on his leg. A dark figure emerges from the overgrowth by the stream, and my hackles rise and I bare my teeth. "Easy now, Maya. You don't want to start a fight with this one."

I shift and throw my dress on before the stranger gets too close. My eyes trail over his muscular frame and the blue streaks adorning his skin. I've never seen anything like this creature before.

"I just finished some venison chili. Why don't we try a bowl?" Mom announces. The man nods and follows her inside.

"Who is he?" I whisper to Dad.

"That is a Guardian."

My eyes shoot to the man's departing silhouette as I recall that the Guardians are meant to protect and keep the peace. "Why is he here?"

"Unfortunately, we upset Luna's balance when we attacked the Fangs pack in Carson City, and he is here to discipline the guilty." He waves off my shock as we enter the house. "Don't worry. I won't let anything happen to you."

I sit at the table and stare as the Guardian digs into his bowl. "Why do you need to eat? I mean, aren't you super powerful?"

His icy eyes meet mine. "We are like any other being. We eat and sleep regularly."

"Can you die?" I blurt out. My dad coughs on his spoon and Mom dabs her mouth.

"Why, Maya? Are you trying to plot something else?"

His implication sends chills down my spine. "I don't understand. What do you mean by something *else*? What have I plotted before?"

"Weren't you a member of Spike's pack?"

"Not exactly."

"What do you mean? Didn't you travel to their ancestral gathering, drink with them, and in turn, pledge your loyalty?"

"Well, yes, but at the time, I didn't know what that meant."

"And didn't Spike ask you to be his mate?"

I shake my head of the haunting memories. "How do you know all of this?"

"I've been compiling evidence from others."

"*Evidence*? Do you think I'm some kind of criminal?" His lack of response confirms it. I can't believe this! I slam my hands on the table as I push back my chair.

"Thank you for the meal. But I'm afraid we should take this outside before Maya embarrasses herself," the Guardian announces to Mom.

I blink as he walks outside without a backwards glance. Dad grabs my elbow. "Maya, I know you are upset, but please calm down. We will take care of this."

I yank my arm free and stomp after the ignorant jerk. I'm not going to let him judge me based on information he *believes* is correct! I pluck a berry off a nearby bush and chuck it at the back of his head. He stops and turns to me with his arms crossed.

"First of all, I never *willingly* agreed to be in Spike's pack. He held a dear friend's life over my head to force my compliance. And when he asked me to marry him, I said no."

"Why did you stay with the Canis pack when the Fangs came for you?"

"Haven't you been listening? Spike is the bad one, so I put him in his place. Why am I being interrogated?"

"Because it wasn't just *his* blood spilt. There were humans among the carnage. And now, the authorities demand that somebody be held accountable."

"The person who is responsible is dead. Your job is done. You're welcome."

The Guardian narrows his eyes while he steps towards me, and the air around us electrifies. "The shifter who's responsible is *not* dead. Not yet, anyway."

"Listen, I never meant to start a war when I went to the Warehouse. I was only trying to rescue Sky. I was trading myself for her *safety*. But Spike also abducted a few women from the Tala pack, and my father had no choice but to get involved."

"So, your father is responsible for the attack?"

"No, of course not."

"Who was the aggressor? Who initiated the dispute?"

"Well, that would be Spike. When he abducted our pack members. As I already stated." He stares at me, unblinking. I rub the bridge of my nose. Is he dense? "What did you say your name was?"

"Everybody calls me the Guardian."

"So, that's your actual name?"

"Azure is my given name, at birth."

"Wait, you were born?"

"Yes, you don't think I materialized from thin air, do you?"

"Does that mean you're human?"

Azure watches a pair of finches fight over a branch above our heads. When they fly into the air, he returns his gaze to mine. "Do you think I'm human?"

"Does it matter what I think?"

A small smile spreads across his face, but he doesn't answer.

"Maya!" Sable embraces me and kisses the top of my head. "I came over as fast as I could. Are you okay?"

I turn towards my accuser, blinking with my mouth ajar. "Where did Azure go?"

"Who the hell is Azure?"

"Azure is the name of the Guardian. I swear he was *right* here."

"Well, wherever he is, I hope he stays there. I can't believe he's accusing *you* of starting this war," he scoffs. "I came to him seeking help to find you, and he wouldn't lift a damn finger. Now, all of a sudden, he's *here*. And because of Spike, of all people."

I pace towards the stream and lean against a tree, watching the water glimmer. Sable rubs my arm and stands beside me. "Azure said humans were killed in the Warehouse. Is that true?" I question.

Sable kisses my hand before moving a lock of hair behind my ear. "We didn't know they weren't shifters. They were fighting side by side with Spike's pack."

A shiver runs up my spine at the thought of innocent people dying.

Then Spike's words pierce my heart. "It's my fault," I whisper as a warm tear falls. "I should let Azure kill me for all those lives lost."

Sable grabs my chin and stares into my eyes. "Come on, Maya. You don't really believe that, do you? Spike took Sky, knowing the consequences. He was asking for trouble."

"I should have just gone back with him when he came to your house. Then it never would have escalated this far."

"And then what? Let him continue to hurt and manipulate you? Hell no."

"Think of how many lives could have been saved if I had."

"Leave the past and all the *what ifs* where they belong—*behind* us. And let's move on to our future."

Storm clouds build above the horizon; the sky is blackening. Sable holds me tight as we watch the sun set in the distance and a cool breeze tosses my hair against my damp cheeks. "Well, I guess it's time to face the music and bury my past."

My leg bounces as we watch Azure converse with the shifters investigating the incident at the Warehouse. He sifts through reports littered with photos. His hands still before he looks over the mess and quirks a brow. "You are shaking the table with your nervous movements." I stiffen my legs, and he returns to the documents. "After talking to the hostages, going over the police reports, and seeing the crime scene, I think I have enough evidence to place judgement. But before I do, I would like to speak to Maya. Alone."

"Like hell!" Sable growls. "It's bad enough you are prolonging this while knowing she is fucking innocent!"

I place an open palm on his thigh. "Please? I just want all of this done and over with." Dad pats my hand and exits without a word.

"I'll be *right* outside." Sable kisses my cheek before glaring at Azure and stomping out.

I stare into my accuser's icy eyes, trying to read his emotions. But he is great at concealing them. Azure leans forward, his gaze never leaving mine. "There is a lot of conflicting data against you. And the humans are demanding justice for the people lost. What would you have me do?"

"The humans never cared before, so *why* now? Those individuals who died in the Warehouse were most likely homeless and beneath them anyway. The only reason they helped Spike was because he cared for them. And, in return, they gave him their loyalty and respect."

"It sounds like *you* cared for Spike."

"In a way, I did. He took me in when no one else would, and he quickly became a father figure to me." There, I said it. It felt good to let it tumble out. Spike was abusive and cruel, but deep down, I did care for him.

Azure reaches his hand out and I stare at it, unsure of his intentions. "If you have nothing to hide, may I read your memories?"

I flinch. Can he really do that? "Why?"

"I would like to understand the situation from your perspective. It won't hurt. I promise." What do I have to lose? I slowly slide my fingers over his. Then he enfolds my small wrist within his, and heat disperses from his touch. "Do I have your permission to access your memories, Maya?"

If this is the *only* way I can prove my innocence, I need to woman up and get it over with. "Yes, you may." Azure offers a comforting smile before he closes his eyes and inhales. I watch as the blue lines across his body shimmer, and a warmth travels up my arm, to my neck, and then spreads across my head. The mystical force sucks me into my memories as if I am reliving them all over again.

It starts with my days at the orphanage and the many beatings I received from my caregivers. Next, I see the happy moments, like when Sara came into my life. I cringe as I stare helplessly, observing a younger version of myself crying over a bloody body before Spike lifts me into his arms. I know what is coming next, and I attempt to pull away from Azure's hand, but I am paralyzed. It's the first night I spent with Spike—when I realized what a monster he really was. I am forced to watch as he beats a man to death with his bare hands, and not just any man but one of the men who killed Sara's mother.

When the reel of my life ends and my eyes flutter open, I am surprised to see Azure holding me. He wipes my tears away with his thumb, and I shudder against the weight of my emotions. "I didn't know I would have to witness my life events all over again. I thought you said it wouldn't hurt."

"Thank you for sharing your past with me. I'm sorry it caused you pain."

"What did you think it was going to do!" I shove him away.

"I didn't know your life was so…"

"Fucked-up?"

"I was going to say *broken*."

"Well, it was." I shake my head, trying to find my equilibrium again. I turn to finish my verbal assault, but my words fail as I see the tortured look on his face.

"Please forgive me. I never meant to hurt you. I was only seeking

187

the truth."

"Well, sometimes the truth is harder to place judgement on, because it's complicated. And like they say, the truth hurts." I stomp past him, but he gently grabs my arm.

"You are cleared of all charges. And I will speak to the humans about Carson City and recommend that they clean up their act, so this won't happen again. I will also stop by the orphanage and speak to the caretakers about their disciplinary policies."

His sincerity stirs my own judgment of him. "You really do care, don't you?"

"Yes, I do, and I'm sorry if I gave you any other impression."

I rub my arms to ward off the chill of my past. "Is it wrong of me to believe that Spike and the others didn't deserve to die the way they did?"

"Of course not. You have a compassionate soul. And even though Spike did horrible things, you still had faith that he could change. That makes you a good person."

"Are we done here? I would really like to see my husband."

"I will walk out with you, but then I need to be on my way." He rubs the back of his neck. "Maya. If you ever need me for *anything*, come and find me. Okay? It's the least I can do."

"How can I find you?"

"Should a situation arise, you'll be able to sniff me out." He boops my nose and smirks. I return the smile as I shake my head. I'm glad he isn't this big scary monster that everybody makes him out to be. He's mostly human, and I almost feel sorry he has to leave. *Almost*. Despite the good that may come out of the experience, I never want to share my memories again.

I let out a breath as Sable embraces me and rubs my back. I cry into his chest, the remnants of my past lingering like a storm cloud. It feels like a burden has been lifted from my shoulders as Azure's verdict sinks in: I'm *innocent*.

Scarlett

Bright Side

After Azure's impromptu arrival and quick dismissal, time flies by as I settle into my new home with Sable and we start our life together. Our marital cave is near my parents, but far enough away to have our own space. *If* you can even call it that, when you have pack members constantly surrounding you. It takes time to adjust, but I am starting to welcome their ever-present hugs, advice, and love. And their happiness rubs off and encourages me to better myself.

So, I attend classes at the university that Phoenix teaches at. As promised, they accepted me without issue, and I'm awarded a generous scholarship to cover my tuition. While my dad and husband offer to pay for my books and lab fees, I turn them down gently and decide to assist Sky at the steakhouse.

Although I never go to Carson City, Celeste tells me there have been major improvements to the orphanage, and it warms my heart to know that Azure was able to get things moving in the right direction before he left.

Even Sara is flourishing in this new environment. She has completely blended into her adoptive family and visits with me and the pack often. Her mother teaches her the ways of her people and how they coexist with the environment around them. Sara catches on fast and enjoys learning.

"I'm so proud of you."

I blush as I pull my cap off. "Thank you, Dad."

Sable kisses my cheek. "So, have you decided what position you want to take?"

"Let me enjoy my graduation first, then I'll worry about what to do with the diploma."

"Maya!"

"Sara! I'm so glad you could make it. Wow! You need to stop growing. You're as tall as I am in those heels."

"Tell me about it. I'm almost thirteen and taller than everybody in my grade. It's embarrassing."

"You are just growing quicker than your peers. There's nothing wrong with that. You are *beautiful*. I love that color on you, by the way. It matches your eyes."

Aspen scoffs, "How is it that females are allowed to compliment each other like that, but men aren't?"

I quirk a brow. "You want to compliment a man *like that*, Aspen?"

"I didn't say that." He blushes. "I just meant, if I were to say that to a woman, she would think I was hitting on her. But you say it, and it's cool."

"And that's why you're still single." I smirk at him.

I lean on a lawn chair as the fire crackles in the middle of the field. I sip my wine and sigh.

"What are you thinking about over there?" Sable questions.

"How much my life has transformed over the past four years. And how grateful I am that I met you."

"Are you trying to get into my pants?" I laugh and shake my head in response. "I couldn't imagine a life without you, Maya. You are my world." He kisses me gently and we both hold hands while watching the embers shimmer. Sky and Freddy dance near the flames, stripping their clothes off as they go.

"Have you noticed Sky has gained weight?"

"Isn't that against the rules? Questioning a woman's weight?"

"Have you noticed the shape of her stomach?"

Sable squints. "It doesn't look like belly fat to me."

I grin and elbow him. "Good deduction, Sherlock."

He frowns at me. "What am I missing?"

"I might be wrong, but I think your sister is expecting."

"Expecting what, exactly?" I stare at him, waiting for him to catch up on my meaning. I watch the emotions pass over his face before he leaps and runs across the field. "Son of a bitch!"

I laugh as he slams into Freddy and roars at him. Once they duke it out, we move the party back into our cave home.

"Sky could have told me," Sable grumbles.

"Sable, your sister doesn't have to tell you *everything*. It's her body. Her choice."

"But they aren't even married."

I kiss the top of his head and wrap my arms around him. "I'm sorry she didn't confide in you, sweetheart. And I promise, when I get pregnant, you will be the first to know."

Sable pulls me into his lap on the bed and nuzzles against me. "I can't wait for that moment." He glides his hand up my thigh, and my breath hitches. I hum softly as my palms rove over his biceps. Then he slips two fingers between my folds and moves teasingly slow. "I know we agreed to wait to have pups, but I do love to practice." I crush his lips with mine, and we are all teeth and tongue while I move my hips, encouraging his digits to move quicker and harder. Sable eagerly jams another finger inside and picks up the pace. "You are so wet," he growls against my shoulder. "Are you going to come with just my fingers?"

When he bites my neck, I moan and lean back to give him full access. "You have been depriving me."

His movements stop as he stares at me with wide eyes. "I *what*? You are the one who has been running your ass off with school and work. Then, when you come home, you crash. If anything, *you* are depriving *me*." Sable makes a great argument. I have been consumed with my studies. But that's over now.

Grabbing his wrist, I pull his fingers out from my core and to my lips. Then I suckle each digit clean. "I'm sorry. Let me start making it up to you." I kneel in front of him, sucking his erection into my mouth. I swirl and taste him until he is sweating.

"Damn," he grunts out, massaging my scalp and encouraging quicker motions. With his free hand, he tweaks my clit. I moan against his throbbing member as he strokes me just right. We both come at the same time, then collapse back onto the bed.

"I don't want you to feel bad about going to school." Sable breathes out as he kneads my breast. "I'm proud of you, and I have no regrets about our life."

I push into his hands as he pinches my nipples. "I have no regrets either."

Sable slams into my juicy center. Then we ride each other until we scream our combined releases and fall asleep in a tangled mess of limbs.

I jump from my slumber when I hear a knock on the door. At first, I think I'm dreaming, but then I hear it again. I grumble as I pull on Sable's shirt and answer.

"Your father has requested your presence."

I rub the sleep from my eyes and motion for Jackson to come inside. "Can I have coffee first?"

"Maya, this is serious. Coffee will have to wait." The beta is always so stern. Why Dad likes him, I'll never know.

"Fine. Have it your way. But if I get cranky, it's *your* fault." I stab a finger into his chest.

"Does he need me too?" Sable scratches his stubble.

"You can come along, but he only requested Maya."

Sable pivots towards the bedroom, but I yank him back. "Oh, no. If I don't get coffee, then neither do you. Let's go."

"But he only wants *you*."

"We are a team, remember? Until death do us part."

"Pfft. Frost probably just wants to ask why we haven't popped out any kids yet."

"I explained our five-year plan to him, and he understands we want to wait."

"Then why is he always giving me shit about it?"

"Because he is getting older and more forgetful."

"Well, he warned me if I can't *perform,* then he's pushing Jackson into my place to make sure the job gets done."

"Stop it. My dad wouldn't do that," I scoff. "Besides, he knows Jackson wouldn't be able to handle me."

"You know, I'm standing right here," the man in question grumbles, as we all head towards the assembly room.

"We know," we say in unison.

"And I *would* be able to handle you." He winks my way.

"You would have to catch me first, and hope I didn't slit your throat for putting your nasty paws on me."

"Well, I do like it rough."

Sable wraps an arm around my waist. "All right. That's enough, you two. Nobody is slitting throats or getting it rough."

"Sable, I'm surprised by your inappropriate conversation with my daughter." Dad glares as we approach him.

I snicker. "Yes, my virgin ears cannot handle such nonsense, darling."

Before Sable can respond, Dad motions us into the conference room. "Everybody, have a seat, please."

I hug my mom, then slide in next to her as Sable lowers himself beside me. I scan my surroundings and frown as I notice we aren't alone. There are also pack alphas from three nearby territories among us. Dad waves to the closest male, allowing him to speak first.

"Thank you for assembling on such short notice. We are in dire need of your assistance. Members of our pack have been disappearing."

The room is overcome by silence, and I lean forward, holding on to his every word. He explains that his pack has dwindled from fifteen to ten. The members go off for a hunt or exercise and are never seen again. And the only leads have been some tire marks near the areas they were last seen, but nothing has come of it.

"We will be vigilant and tighten our border patrol. Thank you for letting us know."

"Actually, we came to ask for your help."

"What is it you need from us, Robert?" Dad prompts.

"We want to combine our packs and grow our numbers for protection."

Everybody starts murmuring amongst themselves.

"Robert, you know how dangerous that is. With that many males in one pack, there will be trouble."

"Yes, but we are running out of options."

My dad leans back and rubs his chin. "Have you tried to contact the Guardians?"

"Since we are unsure as to what is happening to the missing wolves, we don't want to bring them in yet. Considering your experience with lost pack members, we were hoping you could offer us some advice."

I feel everybody's eyes on me, and I flush.

"My daughter was taken by a shifter seeking vengeance. Do you have anybody who fits that description?"

"No, we don't."

"Then I'm sorry. I cannot offer any more advice on the matter."

"So, you won't help us?"

"I never said that."

"But you won't let us combine packs?"

Dad massages his temples. "It's too dangerous. I'm sorry. But, if you want to send over your women and children until this threat is taken care of, I will allow it."

Robert jolts up, slamming his hands on the table. We all stare wide-mouthed at the outburst. This is the very reason Dad is against the man's proposition. It's written all over Robert's contorted face. His inner wolf is threatened by the idea of taking away his family, even if it is for their protection, because he wants to be the one to defend them. But he knows he can't.

My chest aches for him and the hopelessness he must be feeling. I reach for his hand, but he glares at me. Then our eyes meet. He shakes his head and releases a breath. "I'll take your offer into consideration, Frost."

I watch with a heavy heart as he slumps out of the room with the other pack leaders. When the door closes, I pivot to Dad. "They could lose their entire pack. Isn't there something else you can do?"

"Maya, your compassion warms my soul, but I can't allow it."

"You saw them... they came here with their tails between their legs, *begging* for assistance. You have to realize our safety also depends on theirs, because we are closely linked," Sable adds.

"Enough! I have dealt with too many alphas in one area before. And only death comes of it." When he sees my mouth ajar, Dad narrows his eyes and throws an alpha command at us. "We will *not* speak of this again. My decision is final."

My lips clamp shut and I storm out with a glare shot in his direction. He has been coaching me for years, urging me to be *more* considerate of pack members, even providing me with opportunities to step up and give some alpha commands in his absence. So, why did he shut me down so quickly? The sting of his rejection hurts more than I care to admit.

When I turn the corner, I skid to a stop, plowing into Robert while he takes a drag from his cigarette. The corner of his lip quirks at my raised brow, and he flicks the lit end. "It's *not* a habit I'm proud of. But in times like these, the compulsion is hard to ignore."

We stand shoulder to shoulder, lost in our own thoughts, while birds flutter in the fields and enjoy the early spring blossoms.

"Listen, Robert, I'm sorry about my father's decision. I wish I could persuade him to change his mind, but his sorrow runs too deep."

"I knew it was a long shot, but I had to try." He side-glances me. "Actually, I came here more to see *you*..."

The door opens behind us, and my family files out. There is a cold tension in the air, but I know it will melt soon enough. Sable branches off the group and hugs me. "Are you okay?"

I nod before burying my face into his neck. "I will be."

"Robert, I'm so sorry about your lost family members." Sable shakes the man's hand.

"Thank you. And I do understand Frost's hesitance in offering us assistance, but I was just telling your wife I actually traveled here in search of *her* help."

Sable tightens his grip on me. "What do you mean by that?"

Robert looks around before leaning towards us. "I heard the Guardian owes you a favor."

"The Guardian doesn't *owe* me a thing. He was only doing his job."

"Yes, but rumor has it that when he left, he offered you a favor?" A spark of hope dances in Robert's eyes. He wants this. *Badly*. He needs this. I rub the back of my neck as I consider the situation. Could I hunt down the Guardian? Would he return with me? I mean, Robert already mentioned that there were *no* indications that humans were disrupting the peace. "I'll understand if you don't want to use your freebie on *us*. We are mere strangers to you, but I had to ask. It was my last hope."

"It's *not* that. I would gladly assist if I knew the Guardian would be able to help in this instance. But I'm not sure the matter qualifies for his intervention."

"Well, did he mention any stipulations?"

"No, he didn't."

Sable steps forward. "We do want to help, but the last time the

Guardian got involved, a lot of pain came from it. Why don't you leave us your phone number, and we will call you when we've come to a decision?"

Robert's face falls and the sparks in his eyes dissipate—an expression that's all too familiar to me. I step forward with my chin high. "I'll do it for you." Both men stare at me with mixed emotions. I swallow my reluctance before I chicken out. "Robert, gather some clothing from the missing pack members, and I will do my best to hunt down the Guardian."

"You have no *idea* how much I appreciate this. I'll meet you with what you need. At the ancestral grounds. In two hours." Robert takes off at a jog before shifting and galloping towards his territory.

"Are you sure about this, Maya?"

"Of course I'm not. But did you see the life return to his eyes? It's worth it. Even if I have to track down those individuals myself."

"Your dad will never allow it."

"That's why I won't ask for his permission." I slap my mate on the back as I pass, but he snatches my wrist.

"Wait. You can't just take off without telling him."

"I'll leave a note, and by the time he reads it, I'll be gone."

"Well, what if I don't allow you to leave?" The statement slaps me across the face. Sable has never restricted me before, so why now?

"What would you *expect* me to do?" I hold my breath. What would I do if he demanded I stay? Would I still help Robert and his family, or comply with my husband's wishes and regret it for the rest of my life?

"You are so damn stubborn," he grumbles. "I'll make arrangements to travel *with* you, because you sure as hell aren't going alone.

"Thank you for understanding. I'm very fortunate to have you in my life."

"Just keep stroking my ego like that, okay? It doesn't make my wolf happy to allow you to *play* alpha."

I grin. "I will stroke you all night long."

He intertwines our hands and tugs me towards our home. "Why wait? We have two hours to kill."

Sable

Stroke It

"**W**ho are you talking to?"

I hold a finger up to Maya, before placing the caller on speaker phone.

"I'm sorry, Sable. I tried." I rub my temples as Carly cries through the receiver—she's despondent over Sky and Freddy's relationship. I've let it go, especially since Sky is pregnant with *his* pup and seems to be happy.

"Carly, just give it time," I grit my teeth as she throws obscenities my way. What the fuck is wrong with this woman? It's not my fault! I'm not my sister's keeper!

Maya rolls her eyes before she snatches the phone out of my hand and leaves the room to chat with the crazy she-devil. I lean back into the couch and groan.

Before Freddy, Carly and Sky were tighter than best friends. Hell, I'm certain if Luna's laws allowed it, they would have had a *family* together by now. I can't say I blame them. I'd rather have pussy over dick any day. But I'm partial. I have an amazing wife.

The sobs grow softer, and I glance around the corner. Are they done? This is supposed to be sexy time with my damn mate. But like an idiot, I answered my phone—though, in my defense, I worried something was wrong with Sky when I saw Carly's name flashing across the screen.

Thinking about Maya and how she stood up to her dad today brings a grin to my face. She is really coming out of her shell and becoming the shifter Luna destined her to be: strong, confident, and selfless.

The best part was: I didn't have to say a damn thing, and we were in sync with our verbal attack against Frost. I fear he is losing an important characteristic of being an alpha… compassion. Thank Luna my wife has enough of that for everyone. All the trauma she's faced seems to drive her actions to stand up for those less fortunate. At the same time, I worry she may be taken advantage of if she doesn't rein it in and set boundaries.

I agree that something should be done to help find the missing pack members, but running off without a map or an idea of what to do is dangerous, which is why she isn't traveling by herself. I'm going to be glued to her side like her fucking shadow. Plus, the fresh air and alone time sound incredible. No schoolwork, no tool tinkering, and no alpha duties. Just Maya and me, running wild in the woods. I can already taste her as she writhes beneath my feasting mouth. And hear her screams of ecstasy as I pound into her. I adjust myself and glance into the other room again as Maya hangs up with Carly.

"So?" I question.

"Carly is worried about the stress Freddy is causing Sky and the baby."

"Women have been through worse and still pop out pups. She'll be fine."

"We should visit with them. You know, check to make sure

everything is good."

I grab her hips, tugging her on the couch. Then I work my hands up her thighs, aching to taste her molten core.

She slaps my hand away. "I'm serious!"

I nip her shoulder before repositioning myself on top of her. I pin her hands above her head and bite her neck. She attempts to squeeze her thighs together, but I put a knee between them. "I'm being serious too. You promised to stroke me all night long," I groan against her nipple.

She arches her neck, filling my mouth with her breast. I release her wrists to torture the other side while I suckle. Just when I think I've finally have her to myself, my phone rings. She wiggles, grabs it with a smirk, and answers. "Hey, Chuck," she sings. What does he want? I sent a text explaining I'd be out of town and that he was in charge of the shop. "Yes, he is right here." She passes the device to me.

"What!"

"I would just like to point out: I need a raise. Especially if I have to keep putting up with your bullshit."

"I covered you when you went on that stupid casino cruise! Then I bailed you out when you got caught with that prostitute. I could have left you in there to rot your limp dick off!"

"Damn, chill. I was just joking."

"Yeah, sure you were." I jolt as Maya runs her hand over my length and bats her lashes. Then she removes my jeans, just enough to pull my member free. "Hey, I got to go, man."

"Is Aspen coming in to help while you're out vacationing?"

Maya licks my tip before suckling the precum. I thrust and close my eyes. Damn, that feels good.

"Are you listening, boss?"

Images of Chuck fill my mind, and I curse and pause Maya's assault. No fucking way am I thinking about my brother or employee right now. "Chuck. Aspen will come in if you ask him to, because he wants the extra cash. Now, I need to go. Don't call me again unless somebody is bleeding or fucking dying."

"Can I bring in Mack to help?"

"As long as you pay him and he has availability." I slam my finger on the end button and turn to my woman. "Where'd you go?"

She walks out of the bedroom with our traveling packs. "Time's up."

"Like hell it is!"

"I promise I owe you, okay?" How many times have I heard that before? Then she falls asleep watching Netflix or while reading one of her smutty novels.

"I only need five minutes, babe." I'm desperate here. My balls are throbbing with need after her little suck show.

"Well, as tempting as that is, I'm going to give you a hard pass. Get it? *Hard* pass?" She laughs as she brushes by. "You'll survive. Come on, big guy, we need to hero up and meet Robert." I'd love to play around and pretend to force her to do what I want, but even after all these years, she can't handle that kind of rough fun. Spike really fucked her up. She'll open up for me... eventually. "How about a deal?" She grins.

"I'm listening."

"You know how you've been teasing my tight hole?" She purrs into my ear as she rubs her ass on my groin.

I hold her against me. "Yes?"

"I'll let you conquer it." I growl as her butt grinds just right. I move my hips and tease that same hole with my tip. "Deal?" she asks breathlessly.

I massage her wrist and place it over my throbbing hose. "For the love of Luna. Either you take care of it, or I will. I can't travel with this hard-on."

Her eyes grow wide as she watches me, and for a second, I worry I may have set off her PTSD. But she surprises me by leaning in and whispering, "How about you get on your knees and beg?"

A tingle runs down my spine as the husky innuendo registers. If my woman needs a little role play, game on. I lower myself to my knees and look deep into her eyes. "Please, Maya, mouth fuck me."

She bites her lip, and I can smell her arousal. "Lie on your back." I do as she asks, my member at full attention and weeping with need. Then she walks to my head and stands over me. I groan as her wet core visibly leaks in my line of sight. "Oh, do you want this?" she asks softly.

"Yes," I demand. She sits on my face, and I waste no time devouring her center. Then she leans towards my stiffness before hungrily taking him in like the best-tasting lollipop, swirling her tongue as she goes. I moan against her lower lips, then continue to please her. As promised, I explode quickly. And soon after, she follows. Then we lie there, panting and enjoying our sweaty mess. "Thank you," I push out.

"No, no, thank *you*."

Scarlett

Seeking

During one of my visits with Sara, she gifted me a traveling bag. At first, I was hesitant that it would weigh me down or hurt my back. But it's an adjustable padded dog pack and fits our shifting needs, because we can easily nudge our muzzle through the rear and slide it on. Then, when we want to access our supplies, we can slip it off the same way.

Inside each bag, we shove: clothes, meal bars, water, money, our phones with solar chargers, and a multipurpose knife that includes a fire starter. Plus, if we are discovered by a human, our names and parents' phone numbers are in bold on the top.

It's been forever since I took a trip with Sable. I've been shut in a classroom for far too long. While the sun warms my fur, I realize how much I miss the forest and the freedoms it offers. Once we get confirmation that Frost is hunting in the northwest quadrant, we leave as quietly as possible to meet with Robert.

"Thank you for coming." I stare into Robert's eyes and nod before he continues. "Here's a shirt from each of our missing members." He stashes them in my zipper pouch. "If you need *anything,* don't hesitate to call. And don't worry, once you get a good head start, I will inform your families of your adventure. Be safe, my friends."

We zoom through the forest, attempting to pick up any scents. I pause and sniff a nearby oak but come up with nothing. Where would the Guardian live? He said I would be able to find him when I need him. My ears pivot as a squirrel scurries into a bush. But other than that, nothing seems amiss. I plop on my fur butt and scratch at my bag. Is this rescue mission a mistake? Should we return home?

Sable drops his bag before he shifts. "Let's take a break. We've traveled far enough that Frost won't be able to spank us." He chuckles as he ruffles my fur.

I grumble but shift. "Azure said I would be able to find him."

"You are putting too much pressure on yourself. Think of this as a game of hide and seek, instead of a rescue mission."

Sable is right. I need to change my perspective. I taste the air as it settles on my tongue. "He is southwest of us, but he is pretty far."

"Well, maybe once he picks up your smell, he will meet us halfway."

"I hope so. Sable, what is my scent like?"

His face brightens with a grin as he brushes a strand of my hair behind my ear. "You are unbelievably intoxicating. You emit a floral fragrance, like a flower garden with so much sweetness, and it's hard not to lick every part of you."

I lean my head on his chest and listen to his heartbeat. "How did I get so lucky?"

"No, I'm the lucky one." He kisses my head. "And I wouldn't have it any other way. You are the ying to my yang." My heart warms as his affection washes over me. I reach up and kiss him softly. "We should continue before we lose more sunlight. Or I decide to pound you into tomorrow," Sable says against my neck. I seriously consider stopping for the day and allowing him full access but decide against it for Robert's family's sake.

After traveling the entire day, we set up camp. I flex my exhausted limbs as I take in the wooded area. "We are getting closer."

"Good, because my feet are blistering." Sable rubs his heels. "And we both need to shower." I wrinkle my nose. He isn't lying. "I smell water not far ahead. Do you want to rinse off before heading to bed?"

"That sounds wonderful." We stride, hand in hand, until we locate a glistening river nestled in tall brush. "Oh, crap. I forgot to grab our camping soap."

"Come on. That's a long walk back. We can go without it."

When did he become so whiny? First, his feet. And now, he's denying me soap because it's too far? Somebody get my husband a pacifier! "*You* might be able to go without it, but as a woman, I have specific *areas* I need to keep clean, thank you very much. Especially if you want to enjoy them later, you gruff, dirty man." I yelp as he uses his body to plant me against a tree.

"What did you just call me?"

I grin into his playful scowl. "I said: you are a *dirty, gruff, old man.*"

"Old!" He nuzzles my neck, sending shivers down to my toes. "Go and grab your soap. And when you return, I'll remind you exactly what this *old* man can do." He slaps my butt, pushing me towards camp.

"I know I packed it. Where the hell is it?" I sift through my belongings but come up empty-handed. I arch a brow at Sable's bag. "If he put it in his bag and didn't tell me, I'm going to kill him." Snatching the fabric, I shove my hands inside the zippered pouch. "There you are. Finally." Stupid thing. Not only did it take a lifetime to find something to use that was environmentally safe, but it had to be smaller than a regular bar.

The breeze changes course and the hairs on the back of my neck tingle before I hear a snarl. I chuck the soap before shifting mid-leap and galloping to the water's edge. As I skid around the bend, I hear laughter before dirt is kicked up in my face. I cough and paw at my burning eyes. Once my vision is clear, I bark frantically as I watch a four-wheeler depart with Sable in the rear. I chase it until he's no more than a dust cloud in the distance.

No. No. No. I divert my gaze from the blood and chunks of fur swirling in the pond. Was he taken by poachers in search of teeth or pelts? I howl for help, then pace as I pant. Was Sable even breathing when they drove off?

Once his scent is gone, I pad back to our site and collapse next to his bag. I whimper into it as I breathe him in like a lifeline. I wail in agony as my heart splinters.

"Come back to me. *Please.*" Memories of the lonely nights at the orphanage threaten to suffocate me. "I won't live without you." Soon, exhaustion and dehydration disable my mind and body. I pray to Luna to take me quickly.

She answers my pleas, and an angel collects me in their arms. I snuggle my face into its warmth. "It's okay Maya. I'm bringing you home." The voice pulls me to reality, and my tear-stained face meets Jackson's.

"No. Put me down. He might come back. I need to stay here and wait." I pound his chest with my fist. "I'm ordering you to set me down. He was only doing this to protect me. It's all *my* fault."

"Shh, relax." His command is soft and laced with concern. "What you have with Sable is special, and he will not rest until he is back at your side." Jackson never falters as he runs through the woods with me limp in his arms. His rhythmic pace lulls me to sleep, while my mind envisions Sable carrying me with promises of love and comfort.

"Why would you take matters into your own hands!" Dad screams. "You had *no* authority to do that!" I pull my comforter closer to my chin while I turn away. "Answer me right now, young lady! Why the hell did you risk your life *and* Sable's?

My mom rubs my back. "I think she has enough regret to last a lifetime, without you adding to it."

"Well, that's too damn bad."

I hear my bed squeak. "I will *not* let you continue to roar at her! Can't you see she's in pain?" Her words fall heavy on my heart. I shove my face into Sable's pillow and sob.

"I will not lose her again, Raven. She is to be under lock and key until I say otherwise. Jackson, you are going to stand guard, and if anything else happens to her, it's your ass." Dad stomps off with my mother yelling at his departing back. I throw the pillow over my head, ready for the world to swallow me whole.

I'm not sure how long my dreams enslave my guilt-ridden conscience. Hours? Days? Weeks? It doesn't matter anymore. Nothing does. But then, someone shakes me awake. I swat at empty air before I chuck a pillow. The assault on my peace stops, until they smack an open palm against my butt. "What the hell?" I spit as I rub my sore cheek.

"I'm not going to sit here and watch you waste away in that damn bed."

"Fuck off, Jackson. You don't get to dictate what I do." I throw the covers over myself again and close my eyes. That's where I see Sable's face again, and I sigh happily. This is the only place I can be with him now. In my mind. In my dreams.

"That's it!" My daydream is short-lived as he throws me over his shoulder like a caveman.

"What the hell? Have you lost your Luna-loving mind? Put me down right now!" I kick until he hurls me into the air. I flail like an overweight chicken before splashing into the stream. The shock causes me to suck in gallons of liquid. I surface, sputter, and spit. My eyes send daggers towards my catapult, because words escape me.

"You need to get off your ass and look around. You aren't the *only* one who is hurting."

I rub my eyes to see my pack gathering to watch the commotion. Concern etches their faces while they step away as I wade in the water. My feet scramble to get a good grip in the muddy bank. When I flop into the stream for the third time, Jackson offers a hand to assist. Once my legs are steady, I wring out my hair. "Pull that shit again. I dare you." As the last word escapes, I smack his chest, sending him backwards with a splash. When he surfaces, I flip him off and saunter away.

My pack surrounds me with hugs; they part to let my dad stride over. We stare at each other until I wrap my arms around his waist. I place my head on his chest and let a tear spill. "I didn't mean for this to happen."

"I know. But you need to be strong for him." He grabs my chin. "We should tell his family what happened."

"No, I can't."

"It's the right thing to do. And they should hear exactly what happened, and why. You owe them that," he presses. Jackson sloshes past us, running his hands through his dripping hair. Dad arches a brow, biting back a laugh. "Jackson, it looks like you have your hands full." The beta stomps away, cursing as he retreats. Once he passes, Dad turns to me. "Maya, be kind to him—for me. He only wants to see you go back to some sort of normalcy."

"I'll never be able to go back to anything remotely normal without Sable. He is my world..."

"I know, sweetheart. I know." Dad rubs my arm while he guides me to my cave. "We are meeting with the Canis family in thirty minutes, and I need to go check on your mother before that."

"What happened to Mom?"

"You mean after she threw a skillet at my head?" He chuckles as he massages his temples. "She needed some space to cool down. She's fine. But I'm sure she wants to be at the meeting, to offer her support. So, I'm going to hunt her down while also staying away from *any* kitchen utensils."

"I'm sorry I caused a fight."

"What doesn't break us will only make us stronger." He pats my back. "Are you going to be okay without me?"

"Yeah, I've been broken plenty of times." I brush off his concern. "Go find your mate."

Dad passes the threshold just as Jackson approaches. "You didn't have to push me in."

I glare while he towel dries his hair. "Are you kidding me? You're lucky that is all I did to you. Now throw some clothes on."

"Thanks to you, they are drying."

"Then I guess I'm meeting with Sable's family without an escort."

Before I can escape, he grabs my elbow. "I was only trying to wake you up. Your pack needs you right now."

"I never asked for your help." I pull back. "And they need me? *I need them*."

"But they can't help if you keep shoving everyone away."

I rub the back of my neck. Nobody can know the pain I'm in, unless I tell them. They aren't mind-readers, although it wouldn't surprise me if those existed. "Go home and get dry clothes."

"I can't."

"Why? Are your legs broken?"

"No, under the circumstances, your dad doesn't want you by yourself right now. And he won't let me leave your side."

"Tell him I made you get clothes. I'm sure he will understand."

"I'm being serious."

"You are *always* serious. I don't think I have ever seen you laugh or even crack a smile. You are all business."

"I laugh and smile."

"When? Name *one* time."

"The barbecue last week. When the teens were chasing that rabbit. Remember that?"

The image of the young wolves chasing a blur of fur passes through my memories. They were panting and failing horribly. Then, suddenly, the prey jumped into a hole near an oak tree. The shifters couldn't stop fast enough, and all three of them collided with the stump. "That was pretty funny."

"See? I can laugh. Why don't I just borrow some of Sable's clothes. I think we are about the same size."

"No." My tone stops him in his tracks. "How about we go to your cave, so you can collect some? I'm sure you'll be more comfortable in your old-fashioned attire anyway."

The walk to his home isn't far, but the silence is thicker than the morning dew. Once we get close, I move out of the way so he can open the door. When I shuffle past the entrance, I glance around the small home with its beautiful nature and portrait paintings and huge bookcases. As I peruse, Jackson returns, buttoning up his pants and throwing on a shirt. "Happy?"

"Not really, no. But thanks for asking." I run my hand over a portrait of a man and woman bouncing a baby in a grassy field. I squint at the signature. "Where did you get this one from?"

"I made it. Now, let's go."

"You? No way."

"We are going to be late if you don't pick up the pace."

"If you are the artist, then tell me *who's* in the painting."

"It's you and your parents, just before your first birthday."

I scoff, "You aren't old enough to have painted that."

"I have a very good memory. When your parents lost you, I witnessed their pain firsthand. I was left with the urge to make them *something* to help them feel better. So, that's what I made."

"Then why do you have it, instead of them?"

Jackson stops speed walking, and I slam into his back before he faces me. "Because it hurt them too much to remember that precious moment." His reply knocks the wind out of me. How much turmoil had they underwent, to reject such a heartfelt gift? I steal a glance into his eyes. And how much did it hurt to create a masterpiece, only to have it cast aside? "Can I have it?"

The wheels turn, and just when I think he's going to outright bark at my request, he pivots. "We'll see." He starts walking again. "If you behave yourself and don't kill me while I sleep, I'll consider it."

His lighthearted banter softens the atmosphere. "No promises." My hand lingers over the conference room door. As the metal touches my skin, I jerk back. "I can't do this. I can't tell them."

I pivot to hightail it back the way we came, but Jackson catches me. "I know you want to run from this pain. But you need to find it within yourself to be brave. They need to know. And you won't be doing this alone. We are here for you. For support..." He grabs my chin and forces me to look into his eyes. "Man up, Little Wolf." Then he pulls his lips back into a smile.

I wrinkle my nose. "I lied. Don't smile. You look like a creeper." He chuckles as he opens the door and pushes me through. At the sudden force, I trip but catch myself. When I look up, I see everybody staring.

Celeste strides over and grabs my hands. "Your dad said you needed to tell us something." She smiles while tears brim her eyes.

"Has it finally happened? Are you and Sable expecting?"

Talk about a double whammy. The happiness in her voice makes my heart crack. I never knew she wanted grandchildren that much. I wrap my arms around her. This is the part I can't do—give the news that will inevitably crush them all. "I wish it was that simple, Celeste."

"Why don't we all have a seat?" Dad suggests.

I can't meet their gazes. Warm tears coat my cheeks. When I gather enough courage, I tell them how Sable and I snuck off to track down Azure, and how my mate was attacked.

"No." Celeste's hands shake as they cover her mouth. "My baby boy. Please tell me it's not true."

"I'm afraid I can't," my dad whispers. "I'm sorry. We have teams of our best trackers out there looking for him, but they haven't found any leads. I had hoped to give you better news…" His sentiments are drown out by her cries—her pain will forever haunt my nightmares. Celeste opens her mouth to speak but runs out of the room wailing instead. Aspen and Sky rush to follow her.

"Do we know if they were shifters?" Phoenix's voice trembles as he holds his head high.

"I'm not sure. I got their scent and faces before they drove off. But they were unfamiliar. I'm so sorry. It's all my fault. I should have just gone by myself. Then he would still be here."

Phoenix holds me as I cry into his chest. "Sable loves you so much, Maya. Do not blame yourself. He wouldn't want you to live like that."

"We can make funeral arrangements as soon as your family is ready," Dad says softly.

My heart stops. My eyes dart to him. "What? But we aren't even sure if he's dead!"

"I never suggested it had to be an immediate event," my dad soothes. "But with the amount of blood we found…"

"Stop. Don't look at me like *that*. My husband could still be alive. *He could*." I stare into Phoenix's eyes. "You're his father. You can't give up. Let me go to the Guardian. He owes me. I can demand that he find Sable for us."

"No, Maya," my dad commands. "This is how you got into this mess, by chasing after that damn Guardian." His meaning slaps me across the face, and I purse my lips.

Phoenix turns to my dad. "We will assist in the search and keep you posted. Thank you for your help." Then he departs with slumped shoulders.

"Please, Dad, if you'd just let me search… I was so close before all of this happened."

"Maya, no. The sooner you come to terms with everything, the better."

"Come to terms with what?"

"With the fact that your husband and the other missing shifters might be dead, and that there's probably nothing we can do about it, except make sure it doesn't happen to anybody else. We are tightening up our border patrols and alerting the Native Americans and authorities of our situation and have asked for further assistance."

"I can't just sit here and do nothing when my mate is in danger."

"I love you, and it pains me to see you like this. Grief is a heavy burden to bear. But Luna will look after the lost ones now. And you must move on with your life."

"I can't, Daddy."

"Yes, my dear, you can. And you will."

Scarlett

Peace

My mate's bond to me has disappeared. Now there's an ache, a feeling of missing something I never realized was there to begin with. I aid in the search and rescue until I pass out from exhaustion every night for weeks. The number of volunteers dwindles over time. Then it's just my family and in-laws searching. In all my travels, I never again catch the scent of Sable or even Azure.

None of this makes sense. The other lost shifters vanished from their last known location. But my husband left a trail of gore. Was there more than one creature after us? Whatever is going on, I dread what's coming next.

"Thank you all for being here. Today, we are gathered to say goodbye to our brother, Sable Canis..." My dad's words drone on while I gaze at the picture of my mate's face. My mom squeezes my hand as she dabs her eyes. I tune out the noise and close my lids. And in that darkness, there's my husband again, living inside my sweet daydreams. Wrapping me in a hug. Kissing me. Telling me how much he loves me. I can't say goodbye…

After the ceremony, I escape to my den. I slouch at the table and knock back my liquid comfort. The burning sensation can't begin to match the pain inside my heart, but it's a start. Realizing the numbness I seek remains elusive, I chuck the meaningless glass and watch as it shatters into shards.

"Are you done with your pity party?" Jackson grumbles as he collects my mess.

"Why don't you say that to my face, pretty boy?" I hiccup. There is a knock on the door, but I rest my head on the table to escape the pounding. Jackson strides to the entrance. I reach for his arm. "Just ignore it. Maybe they will go home." I hear the door open and I groan.

"Maya, I'm so sorry." Sara wraps her arms around me and wets my shirt with her tears. "Sable rescued us, and now he's gone." I rub her back as my lip quivers and I stare into space. I've always been the one to hold Sara when she sobbed. Now that the tables have turned, it feels awkward. "What can I do to help?"

I peer into her eyes, and my sarcastic bark falls. This is my Sara. She's like a daughter to me. "Any way you can go back in time?"

"If I could, I would have done it already. Jackson, tell me what needs to be done?"

"She smells pretty raunchy."

"Look who's talking?" I gripe. Sara giggles, then tugs me into my room and closes the door. I sit on the bed as she draws a bath. "Sara, he was just being an ass. I don't smell bad."

"Hey, it gives me an excuse to hang out and catch up on gossip. Plus, I'm only doing what you did for me." Once the basin reaches capacity, she guides me into the sudsy tub. I settle under the hot liquid before she scoops up the contents and washes my hair. While she massages my scalp, I realize how much this girl likes to talk. She gabs about anything and everything under the sun. When she loses steam, she props up her phone and we chortle over a mindless techno chicken video.

As the water chills to the point of being uncomfortable, I step out and dry before Sara braids my hair over my shoulder. Then she applies makeup to my cheeks. The routine brings peace into my heart and reminds me of our time together at the orphanage. Those were dark days, moments I *never* imagined I would get through. "There. You look and smell more like yourself!"

I pivot and pucker my crimson lips at my reflection. "This lipstick is too much. I look like a whore."

"Oh, I'm sorry. You aren't?" My mouth falls open before I begin tickling her. Her giggles dance around and brighten the room. "Stop! I'm going to pee my pants!" she hollers.

We fall back onto the bed. It feels good to cry from laughter. "Thank you for coming over, Sara."

"Of course. I'm here for you whenever you need me. Now get up."

"Why?"

She pulls an airy material over my head and forces me to twirl. The baby blue sundress flies around my waist before settling at my knees. "You'll see."

We walk, hand in hand, into the warm night towards rows of candles that lead to a large oak tree. I place my palm over the thick trunk. "This tree has been here longer than we have and will remain long after," Jackson says from beside us as he pats the bark. "The Native Americans believe that its roots grow to the center of the planet, which allows us to communicate with our loved ones in the beyond. When a pack member passes on, we mark its trunk and guide the spirits with candlelight. Then we dance around its branches, hoping that it will encourage the spirits to join us."

I run my finger over the many tick marks carved in the wood. "It's a beautiful thought, right?" Sara offers with a smile.

"Do you really believe all that crap?"

"Why not? It brings hope to those who need it the most. And I would like to think my mom can hear me. I mean my real mom."

I blink, confused. "Your mom is still living, Sara," I continue the lie I've been telling her for years.

"You don't have to pretend anymore to protect me. Debbie told me what happened to my mom."

"I'm sorry, Sara."

"Don't sweat it. Besides, I can just pick a branch and dial her up." She tugs on the lowest tree limb and pretends it's a phone. Then we burst into a fit of giggles. I turn my head as a violinist plays from the shadows. The music is calming, and I find my hips swaying lazily. The candles flicker as everybody grabs a partner and moves to the melody. My parents lean their foreheads together and grin into each other's eyes, and my heart aches. Even Sara finds a partner to dance with.

"Maya?"

I lift my chin at Jackson as he offers me a hand. "I don't know."

"Don't tell me you find dancing intimidating?"

"No."

"So… you find *me* intimidating?"

"Hell no."

He grasps my hand and tugs me to him. I squeak before putting distance between our bodies. Then I clear my throat, unable to look at him. "You *are* intimidated by me."

"Pfft. You wish, beta."

"Look at me, Maya." I peer into his amber eyes. "See? I'm not that scary."

"I never said you were."

"Your eyes tell me differently."

"I… I don't feel comfortable being this *close* to you."

"I just thought you needed a friend right now." He takes a step back and shoves his hands into his pockets.

"I appreciate all your help."

"No. I get it." He walks off into the night. "I'm going to get some air."

I can't help but watch until his frame is consumed by the velvety blackness. "Do you know why I chose him to watch over you?" Dad rubs my back and I lean in to him. "He lost his mate early in life. He only had five years with her. Then she died giving birth to their child."

"I never knew."

"Maybe if you were *willing* to listen, he would tell you one day."

"I am always willing to listen."

"Do you really think so? I mean, you have been understandably preoccupied ever since you came back to us… between Sable, college, and working at the steakhouse. I'm not trying to guilt trip you. I know a lot has happened in your short life. But don't get so caught up in what's going on *inside* your head that you lose your connection with those surrounding you. One of the greatest gifts we can give to others is our *time*. And we never know how much of it we have left—the present is so precious."

"Sorry to interrupt, but Debbie is here to pick me up, Maya. And I didn't want to leave without a proper goodbye."

"Thank you again for coming, Sara. Don't be a stranger. I love you."

"I love you too."

After we embrace, she skips off to Debbie. I wave as they depart, then a faint glow catches my attention. I pivot and notice Jackson's lights are on in his house. I drag my feet before knocking and waiting for an answer. When it doesn't come, I push the door open to glance around. "Hello?"

The smell of paint smacks me in the face, and I cough. How anyone can be surrounded by the odor is beyond me. My ears perk up as I notice music playing. I stick my head inside the room it's coming from. I scan the contents, until I pause on Jackson sitting on a stool and painting large strokes over a wrapped canvas. I step over the threshold but halt at the sight of him completely naked with paint splatters adorning his thighs. But that's not what stops me in my tracks. The painting is like a magnet drawing me in. When I approach, he snatches his earbuds out. "I'm sorry. I didn't hear you come in."

I reach towards the fresh brushstrokes as tears smear my makeup. "It's beautiful." My eyes trail the image of Sable and me, the ceremonial cup in my mate's hands as he grasps it from mine with a soft twinkle in his eyes. "You recreated this from memory?"

"Yes." He blends his brush to darken the night sky.

"Can I watch you paint? I promise I won't bother you." I locate a vacant corner before sitting cross-legged on the floor, mesmerized and eager to witness his masterpiece unfold. He silently pivots, pops his earbuds back in, and gets messy.

Sunlight filters in from a nearby window, stirring me from a restless slumber. I stretch my sore limbs and groan at the kink in my neck. My fingertips dig into the muscle, begging it to stop twitching. My eyes focus, and I gasp. Like a siren, the finished painting beckons me forward and I kneel at its base. Lifting a shaky hand, I trace the colorful scene.

"Good morning, sleeping beauty."

While I swipe at my eyes, I feel the steam of a hot beverage under my nose. "Thank you." Jackson brushes past me before staring out of his window into the early morning light. The same sun I was just grumbling at for ruining my sleep I'm now praising as it gleams off his frame. I flush and look away, unsure why seeing him nude *this* time is so different from all the others. I clutch the mug as I side-glance his unmade bed. Maybe it's because I'm in his bedroom? I sip at the liquid to distract myself but gag on the charcoal water. "What is this crap?"

I hear him chuckle, never shifting his eyes from the glass pane. "It's called coffee."

"This is *not* coffee. It's bird shit in a cup." I snatch his mug.

"Hey, that's mine," he protests, trying to grab it back.

"If you spill scalding coffee on me, I will *never* forgive you."

"As if you have ever forgiven me for anything."

"I *have* forgiven you." I sip his coffee and glare. "You gave me *black* coffee and made your own with cream and sugar."

A slow grin spreads over his face. "Because you are sweet enough." He pinches my cheek.

"Ouch!" I kick him away. Once he is at least six feet from me, I pivot to the window and sip his coffee. I smirk as I watch a group of young wolves biting and clawing each other in a dog pile. One of them stops and wags his tail at us. Jackson lifts his hand up and waves at the pup. "Aw, Ash really likes you." I elbow him. "You finally found *somebody* who does." I offer him another smirk. But it fades as I see the lost look in his shimmering eyes. I touch his hand, pulling him back to the present. "Here, you can have your coffee back, if it means that much to you."

He clears his throat and walks out of the room. "It's not the coffee."

I follow him to the kitchen and sit at the table, waiting for him to explain. I feel the air around us thicken. "Do you want to talk about it?"

"Listen, I'm sorry I didn't put cream and sugar in your cup. I need to go shopping. I just haven't had much free time."

"Forget the coffee. I meant do you want to talk about your wife." The mug slips from his fingertips and crashes, sending ceramic shards sliding across the floor. We bend down at the same time. "I'm sorry... it's none of my business. Ouch. Stupid glass." I suck on my injured pointer finger.

"Let me see that." He wraps my hand in a towel. "Her name was Ashely, and she was breathtakingly beautiful but very quiet and easily overlooked." He pauses and gets lost in his memories. When some time passes, I squeeze his palm, urging him to continue. "We married young, and right away she became..." He swallows. "... pregnant. We were so happy and excited. But then she lost the child.

Time and time again, this happened, until one day she made it past the six-month mark. Then the eighth. It was a miracle. We finally got to hold our baby boy and it was heaven on earth. Then she started hemorrhaging and her heart rate dropped."

My hand covers my gasp as his pain stabs me in the gut. When Sable and I were married, we agreed to wait to have children— until I had a career and our lives were more stable—but now my heart aches at the thought of not having a piece of him to hold and cherish.

"I miss her. Her presence was so calming."

"I'm sorry. I don't know what to say."

"You know how it feels. You know there are no words to soothe the loss."

"Was Ashely buried with your son?"

"My son is still alive and well."

I blink, not sure if I heard him correctly. "What do you mean? Where is he?"

"You have to understand, after my wife died, I was beside myself with grief... so a couple from the pack, who couldn't have children of their own, adopted him."

"Oh..." I draw out. So, that's why he has been so hard on me about moving on? Because he didn't, and in his misery, he gave up the opportunity to be a father to his son...

"Go ahead and dish out your judgements. I know how horrible it sounds."

"I wasn't going to *say* anything."

"Well, that's a first." The comment stings. I brush past him to stride outside, not wanting him to see the hurt on my face. The warm sun attempts to lift my mood. Suddenly, a soccer ball flies overhead.

"Whoops, sorry." Ash runs over to grab the ball. Then he tosses it to me with a grin. "We are short one. Want to make it even for us?"

"Sure, buddy." I throw the ball in the air and then twirl it on my pointer finger.

"Ash, what did we agree to? No girls allowed!" Aspen smirks from the other team. I narrow my eyes before flipping him off. The kids gasp, and I cringe at my inappropriate gesture.

"Maya did something bad," Ash tattles to Aspen.

"We need to tell the alpha so he can spank her." He smirks.

"Are we here to play or talk?" I fling the ball to Aspen, and he lets out a breath as it hits him in the chest. He narrows his eyes and the game is on. I rein in my aggression as the children gather around me to steal the ball. After my muscles have warmed, my mood improves.

"It's time I head home, guys," Aspen announces. "It was great seeing you again, Maya. Don't be a stranger." He hugs me tight.

"We are down one now." Ash scans the field. "Hey, Dad! Come and play with us!"

I turn wide-eyed as Jackson jogs over. Then I pivot back to the boy. Is *Ash* his child? Ash's giggles ring out as Jackson picks him up and tosses him in the air. "I don't think she can handle a professional like me, son."

"Whatever. You are so full of yourself. You're not professional at anything, except eating."

The game goes well, but Jackson steals the ball from me at every turn. My competitive side boils over, and soon we tumble in the grass after we collide. "Get off me, fatty," I grumble.

"You're the one who ran into me, lard ass."

"Dad, you said a bad word." Ash frowns at us before he turns his head as another man calls out to him. The small boy gallops towards the sound, and the other children aren't far behind.

"Cute kid. Too cocky though, just like you." I try to shove Jackson off.

"Listen, I didn't mean to snap at you. It's still a sore topic." The sun casts dark orange hues over his shoulder.

"If you don't get off me, I'm going to break you, old man."

"Oh, really? I'd love to see that, little girl." My head falls into the grass, and I laugh. "What's so funny?"

"Your face."

"You are *really* trying to get your ass kicked, aren't you?"

"By whom?" He tickles me mercilessly in response. I squeal and thrash around until tears are streaming down my cheeks. "Stop! You win!"

"You're damn right I win." He grins. "And what do I win?"

A male clears his throat behind us, and we crane our necks. "Daddy, *help* me. Jackson won't let me up."

"That's dirty, Maya." Jackson tugs me to my feet.

I brush off the grass and dirt. "Is everything okay, Dad?"

"Robert came by and asked to speak with you." I pale and freeze. "You don't have to. I have no problem telling that backstabber to hit the road."

"No, it's okay. I need to return those shirts anyway." I brush past him before heading home. I bite my lip as I stare at the untouched saddle bags. I lift Sable's and take in his faint scent. What I wouldn't give to see him again… I clutch it to my chest and send a prayer to Luna, before striding out with the borrowed clothing.

"You know, you don't have to do this," Jackson reminds me as we get to the edge of our territory. I clench my jaw and put one foot in front of the other, unable to respond.

Robert embraces me. "Maya, I'm so sorry for your loss. Is there anything I can do for you?"

"You've done enough," my dad growls.

But I ignore him. "I'm sorry I couldn't find your pack members, Robert." I hand him the shirts. "Or reach the Guardian."

Robert clutches the material to his chest. "Thank you. I was just informing your father that we have lost two more members."

"Still no leads or evidence of injury?"

"No. They vanished without a trace."

"I'm sorry."

"Me too. But we won't lose hope." Robert dips his head before leaving us. Where are the shifters going? Who is behind this?

"Maya, dear, are you all right?" My mom rubs my arms.

"Yes," I lie.

"I'm going to the store to get some provisions. Is there anything I can get you, Raven? Frost?" Jackson asks.

"I would love a crystal ball," my dad grumbles at Robert's departing back. "I'd love to get my hands on those responsible."

"I'm coming with you. I haven't been out in a while," I announce.

"Why don't we watch a movie and cook some popcorn, Maya?" Mom runs a hand through my hair, treating me like I'm five years old again.

"You won't let me leave?"

"I didn't say that. I just want to spend some one-on-one time with my daughter." Playing the guilt trip card? Good one, Mom. I can only nod as she guides me to her cave. "I was thinking of a sappy love story. What do you think?"

"Whatever you want, Mom," I groan.

Scarlett

Art to Heart

After three movies, my mom passes out cold on the sofa. I shut off the TV before draping a fleece throw over her. I yawn and stretch, then I stride outside and stare at the moon. Where are the Guardians? Why haven't they stepped in to protect the packs?

"You shouldn't be outside by yourself."

I jump and smack Jackson. "I realize that now, especially with creeps like you lurking in the shadows."

"I wasn't lurking," he mumbles as he reads a sheet of paper.

I pluck it from his hands before skimming it. "Wow. An art gallery in Carson City. I never expected that."

"They are searching for a handful of artists to contribute to their huge opening day event, and I was hoping to submit a few pieces."

"That's a great idea."

"Except your dad doesn't want us traveling that far away right now." He shrugs and pockets the paper. "Oh well. Maybe next year. You better get back inside before your mom wakes up and finds you gone."

"Are you going to stay out here all night?"

"Somebody has to keep watch over your crazy ass."

"When are you going to get some sleep?"

"Aw, are you worried about me? And here I thought you didn't care."

I swat his hand away before he can pinch my cheek. Then I stomp inside the house and slump on the couch. My mom stirs and looks around. "Aw, honey, did I fall asleep?"

"Only for a minute, Mom."

She throws the fleece over my shoulders. "You look like you have something on your mind. Do you want to talk about it?"

"Do you know anything about art galleries?"

My mom arches a brow. "Why do you ask?"

"Because I have an idea that can help boost pack morale." We stay up and talk for hours. I learn that my mom was born to another pack and was once a schoolteacher. Then she met my dad and they fell madly in love, before he whisked her away to start a family. While we chat, I make a to-do list for our secret project, and I can't contain my grin.

"It's nice to see that smile again."

"It's nice to have something to do, other than wallow in my own self-pity."

She wraps an arm around me and I snuggle into her. Soon, we drift into a comfortable silence.

"Remind me to *never* sleep on the couch."

"You know there is a perfectly good bed you could have slept in," Dad says, sipping his coffee.

"Yeah, a tiny twin-size. No thanks."

"Then suck it up."

"Thanks for the words of wisdom."

"Anytime, darling."

"Well, everything is all set!" my mom sings, as she walks into the kitchen waving a piece of paper. Then she sets it in front of me. "You just need to find some artists to fill the event with goodies."

I grin at the colorful flyer. "Wow, Mom! That was quick."

"Oh, it was easy, dear. I have been planning events for forever. Now, let me show you how great my *pancakes* are."

It isn't long before the kitchen is filled with the sounds of my parents bickering over the perfect thickness of the pancake batter. I chuckle as my mom flings the pale liquid at dad's face in a fit. He collects her in his arms, and she threatens to dump the whole bowl on his *fat head*. When he dares her, she turns on her heels in a huff. And I watch as the contents drip down my dad's brow and onto his nose moments later.

Mom bites her lip before using the spoon to taste the batter from my dad's cheek. "It's the perfect consistency. I just needed your *hot* air."

241

My dad throws her over his shoulder and stomps out. "Sorry, Maya. But you'll need to make your own breakfast." Their bedroom door closes, and I get the hint.

To save them from the embarrassment, I scamper out and debate whether to go home or see a friend. I knock on Jackson's door, then let myself inside. "If you're naked, get dressed," I call out. "Since *you* went shopping, I'm stealing your food and cooking breakfast."

Once the bacon, eggs, and sausage are all done, I assemble a plate for him and head to his room. I stop short when I realize he's not *alone* in the bed. All I see sticking out of the covers is a perfect set of hot-pink toenails. I stand there, like an idiot, as heat rides up my face. I never expected somebody to be in bed with him. But it makes sense. Jackson is a high-ranking, unclaimed male. And those are hard to come by. I regret wandering in here and decide to tiptoe backwards before anyone can notice me. "Maya? What a pleasant surprise. Don't go, sweetie. I was just grabbing my things and then he's all yours."

"Oh, you don't need to leave." I tilt my head at the woman. "I'm sorry. Do I know you?"

She stands, sending the sheet gliding down her curves while exposing her naked body. "We haven't formally met yet. But I've heard a lot about you from my alpha. My name is Bridgett. I'm from Robert's pack."

Wait… she's from Robert's pack? The same pack my dad is seething mad at? Considering Jackson is second in command, he shouldn't be sleeping with the enemy. If he has an itch to scratch, there are tons of eager, unclaimed females in his own territory.

"Well, there is breakfast in the kitchen if you are hungry. I should really go. I have tons to do." I gulp down air as I push open the front door. Why am I feeling like this? I put a sweaty hand over my fast-beating heart. My wolf yearns to break free, and I let her. I dash past everybody while the grass whips my ankles. The sting is nothing compared to the ache in my heart.

Once my legs are shaking and my breath is coming out in bursts, I collapse in the wildflowers. Butterflies flutter angrily into the air to avoid being crushed. The tall brush covers my fur, and I feel utterly alone. I miss Sable so damn much. My stomach growls, and I whimper at my mistake. I made a wonderful breakfast and forgot to eat any of it. Well, now Bridgett and Jackson can enjoy it together. Approaching footsteps have me cowering against the stalks of greenery. My nose flares, warning me I'm about to get an earful.

"What the hell were you thinking, running off like that?" I turn my head and ignore him. "You know you can't just take off. What if something happened to you? Your dad would kill me." A low growl escapes my throat, and I snap at his foot. "Did you just try to *bite* me?"

I brush past him, flicking my tail against his thigh with a slap before sprinting forward again. I don't need him bossing me around. I'm next in line for alpha, not him. I half-howl, half-yelp as something crashes against my back, and I tumble head over tail down the hill. When I finally stop flipping, I blink into Jackson's wolf eyes. In a show of dominance, he growls and snaps at my neck. I bring my hind legs to his stomach and kick as hard as I can, sending him flying.

"Maya, talk to me!" he shouts once he shifts to two legs.

I follow suit and shove him in the chest. "What the hell are you doing with a female from Robert's pack?"

"You mean Bridgett? We go way back. Before this feud."

"Does my dad know?"

"I don't need his permission. Bridgett is a friend." He grabs my

243

arm as I walk off. "Wow. What is really going on here, Maya. Why are you crying?"

My fingertips slide across my wet cheek. "I'm tired and hungry."

"Well, you made a great meal with my groceries. Why didn't you enjoy it?"

"Because I made it for you."

"Why?"

"That's the same question I have been asking myself." I don my fur exterior and bullet into the valley. This time, I don't stop until I'm home. I slam the door and lock it. Why is this happening? Am I developing feelings for another man? My gaze wanders to my wedding picture hanging on the wall. I run my hand over the frame as my lip trembles. I won't allow him to weasel his way into my heart. I need to get my head straight.

After a scalding shower and cleaning up the house, I feel more like my old self. I laugh at the thought of liking Jackson. I was just tired—that's why I overreacted. Jackson can sleep with whomever he wants. *Pfft. He probably isn't any good anyway. A real waste of man flesh.*

"Maya?" my mom calls from the front door. "Are you okay, dear? I'm sorry your father kicked you out this morning."

I unlock the door to let her in. "I'm fine, Mom. I just needed some time by myself."

"Jackson told us what happened." She pats the couch.

"Oh, so he told you he's sleeping with one of Robert's shifters?" I rub my arms at my mom's arched brows. "Listen, Mom. I appreciate you checking on me, but I need to make some calls and get the event set in motion."

"Well, since you are upset with Jackson, I'm going to keep you company. Dad's orders. Sorry. Unless you want to make up with Jackson and get passed *this*?"

"There's no *this*, Mom. I don't need him breathing down my back every second of the day."

"So you'd rather have your mother?"

"No. I would rather nobody be up my ass 24/7! I'm a grown adult!"

"Then maybe you should prove you are an adult by talking instead of running off." My mom hands me some fliers and sighs. "I'll talk to your dad about removing your security detail. But until then, talk to Jackson. He did nothing wrong, and he has been a good friend."

"Fine." I stomp past her, then stride over to Jackson's house and pound on the door.

He opens it with an arched brow. I straighten and shove a flyer against his chest. "Here. This is for you."

"I don't understand."

"You wanted to go to that stupid art gallery in Carson City, right? Well, I'm bringing the art gallery here, so you can be happy and get what you want."

He leans against the door frame and crosses his arms over his chest. "And why would you do a thing like that?"

"It's a fun event to bring the pack together."

"But you said it was to make *me* happy."

His cocky smirk boils my blood. "Fine, don't come. I'm sure our pack has other artists, just as talented, who would love to enter." I turn on my heels, muttering to myself about what an idiot I am.

245

"How many volunteers did you get?"

"Everybody is really excited and has something to contribute." I stab at a meatball.

"And what about Jackson?"

My meatball flies off my plate. "I don't know."

"Well, did you ask him?"

"Yes."

"And?" my mom pushes out.

"He didn't say if he wanted to come or even enter."

"After all the trouble you two have gone through, he better enter something and be damn grateful," my dad grumbles.

"Dad, this event is voluntary. It's supposed to be fun."

"What are you going to enter, Maya?"

"I wasn't planning on entering anything."

"Why not?"

"I have no artistic abilities… unless you count stealing."

"Why don't you give painting a try? It seems to run in the pack. I have some supplies you can borrow." My mom beams.

"You paint?"

"Before I met your father, I taught elementary school children basic art techniques."

"She was very good at it too." Dad smiles at her. "You should enter something, honey. You would have my vote."

"I have plenty of supplies for us both. Come on, Maya, I'll run over to your cave and get you set up. Then I'll give you a quick lesson." Mom places a tarp on my bedroom floor while she explains basic shapes and techniques and piles up my supplies. "This window is perfect for you."

"What do you mean *perfect*? It's just a window."

"It's not just a window. It is a portal to the world. Your inspiration for your canvas."

I side-glance the pane and snort. "Did you have one too many, Mom?"

"Just enjoy yourself and don't overthink it." She leaves me alone with my blank canvas.

"How am I *not* supposed to overthink this?" I put some red paint on my brush and narrow my eyes at the canvas. Maybe if I just smear every color on there, I can make a rainbow and call it a day? Rainbows are inspirational, right?

"You know, it's not painting itself."

I smell his musk before I see his tall shadow. "Shut up, Jackson."

"You have to relax and simply paint."

"Just go home."

He slumps on my bed. "I can't. It seems your mom is in heat and keeping your dad busy. So I'm here to make sure you stay out of trouble until she returns."

I cringe. Apparently, going into heat is equivalent to taking Viagra. "Gross."

"It's the circle of life, Maya. And our wolves crave that closeness, especially when a female is in heat."

"Nope. Still gross. Especially when you are talking about my mother."

"At least she is married. Loner wolves and unclaimed females have it worse, because every unclaimed male within miles can sniff her out."

"We are *not* talking about this right now." I slam the paint brush down.

Jackson peeks over. "Do you want some advice?"

"No. But you're going to give it to me anyway, right?" His chest presses against my back. "What are you doing?"

"Stop being a baby." He places the paintbrush into my palm. Then he pushes me forward until the bristles rest on the canvas. "Now, make soft *strokes*," he whispers by my ear.

I do as he commands, trying to ignore the effect he is having on me as his breath sends tingles down my spine. "Great job, Picasso. Now I have a line. Thanks, you're a big help."

"Just keep stroking it." He grins against my neck.

"You are turning this into something dirty. Stop it."

"I thought you liked to talk dirty?"

"Not with you."

"Ouch. Why not?"

"Because you have Bridgett for that," I grumble as I slap on some black paint.

"You're right. Bridgett is a wonderful person."

"Oh, I wouldn't know… the only part of her I got acquainted with was her bare chest."

"Well, her back side is superior."

I twist and glare. "You are a pig, you know that, right?"

"No, I'm a wolf." He gives me an all-fang smirk. I pinch the bridge of my nose. This man is grating on my last nerve. "Listen, Bridgett visits once a month, gets what she needs, and leaves. That's it."

"That's a messed-up relationship to have with someone."

"How many times have you been in heat?"

My face flushes and I return to my painting. "We aren't having this conversation."

"Do you realize how hard going into heat is for an unclaimed female wolf? It drives them mad." His hands trail down my arms as he steps closer. "They have an itch they just can't scratch. And the only cure is to find somebody to reach in and take care of business."

My core warms as his palms rest on my hips. His words wash over me like a soft melody to my libido. But this is *Jackson*! "That's ridiculous. Of course, they have control over their actions. And so do you. So, back off."

He sniffs the air, and his grip tightens. "I don't think you want me to do that. I can smell the hormones. Can't you feel them?"

I swallow. Of course I can. *With him this close.* "If you don't remove yourself, I will do it for you." Surprise racks my body as he obeys my request. "Thank you."

"You know, the harder you force down those natural bodily urges, the stronger they will become."

"I doubt that. I have always been in complete *control* during my ovulation."

"But you were also on the pill and that helps tamper down the hormones, so they aren't as strong and more regulated. But now you're not."

He's right. I *was* on the pill... Then, when Sable passed away, I continued with what I had left but never made a follow-up appointment to get my prescription renewed. "How'd you know I was off them?"

"You act like I don't have keen senses." He taps his nose with a wink. "That's why you were so jealous of Bridgett this morning. You thought I wouldn't be able to take care of your needs too. But you're wrong."

"I wasn't jealous."

"Who are you trying to convince? Me or yourself?"

"Even if I can't control my urges, what makes you think I will seek you out to take care of *them*? Remember, I have many options." I smirk at my painting. As next in line, I could choose to roll around in the covers with anyone. Of course, I wouldn't. But Jackson doesn't need to know as much. Let Mr. Cocky-Pants mull over that! Ha!

With one quick stride, he is twirling me to face him. I suck in a breath as I stare into his amber eyes. "Don't do that."

"Do what?" I clench my thighs together.

"Don't act like I'm a pebble in your shoe, one you can easily pick and flick. You may not want me, but don't challenge my wolf by suggesting you will go to another male." His eyes burn, and I know his wolf's ego has been goaded. My words were taken as a challenge. I swallow. A challenge I initiated. I backpedal from the warmth encompassing us. I forget about the paint and lose my footing before falling backwards into the easel and landing on my butt. My mouth falls open as paint splatters the room. The action shifts the tense mood, and Jackson laughs hysterically. "You look ridiculous." He reaches out a hand.

"I'm not touching you! Look what you did!"

"What I did? You were the one saying you wanted to sleep around."

"I *never* said that! I just pointed out that I had options if I couldn't control myself. Listen, I'm more human than animal. I will be fine. But thank you for the, uh, *proposal*. You should stick with Bridgett and her monthly booty calls." I stand and rub my lower back.

"Now this is art."

I turn and see two large circles in the center of the canvas before I notice my paint-covered rear-end. "I ruined it with my big fat ass!"

"It's not ruined. It's unique." I snatch the canvas in response and beeline for the trash can. This is the last thing anybody needs to see: my ass cheeks hanging as décor in the middle of their house. The damaged painting matches the rest of my life. I toss it into the bin, but Jackson grabs it mid-descent. I scowl and reach for it, but he holds the canvas over his head. "It's not destroyed. We can make it a masterpiece. Trust me."

"Trust you? The same person who is trying to convince me that I'm going to turn into a horndog overnight and attack unsuspecting men."

"Not men. One man. And I was volunteering." He grins.

The heat from his body rides up to my cheeks. Maybe I *can't* control myself. I stare at his bare chest, and my hands itch to reach out… I shake my head. "I think you should guard me from outside, Jackson."

"And I thought you were in control?"

"I am, but you keep coming on to me and it's making me uncomfortable."

My words aren't fooling anyone, but he takes a step back all the same. "I'll stop—you have my word. Just remember to keep *your* hands to yourself. Now, let's finish this masterpiece." After an hour of splattering paint around the butt circles, it doesn't look any better. "I love it. We'll call it: *Maya's Butt-tastic Painting*."

A laugh escapes as I set my brush down, pull my hair out of its bun, and shake out my locks. "Whatever you say. I need to shower and head to bed. It's getting late."

Jackson watches me from the door frame. I can tell he wants to spit out another innuendo. But then he smirks and nods. "Have a good night, Maya." His eyes remind me of a hunter. And I'm the meal.

"Are you leaving?" I squeak out.

"*You* tell me. Your body language is *begging* me to come over there and make your wet dreams come true, but your words say differently."

I suck in a breath. How could he tell what I was thinking? "This isn't a good idea, Jackson."

"Of course it is. You get the itch scratched, and my wolf is triumphant." His words splash over me like cold water. He wants to *own* me… just like Spike.

"Triumphant?" I seethe.

"Come on. You know what I mean."

"No, I don't. How about you enlighten me." I cross my arms over my chest. "Is my virtue a trophy?"

"Maya…"

"Oh, I get it. You think the more women you conquer, the more masculinity under your belt. Bullshit. Get out of my house before I kick your ass."

"I never said that. You're putting words in my mouth."

I shove him out the door. "I've dealt with a lot of crap in my life, and I won't be treated like a *toy* you can play with, so you can then brag to your friends about how *triumphant* you were. Not again."

"Wait a minute. I would never do that."

"Just go."

Jackson grasps my shoulders. "Hey, what is going on in that head of yours?"

I can't relive those haunting memories. Not now. Not with him. "Nothing. Why can't I just turn you down and have you accept it?"

"Because there is more to it than that. Who hurt you? Was it Sable?"

"When did I say somebody hurt me?"

"Who was it?" he roars, his eyes blazing.

"Spike."

Jackson holds me tight. "Spike can't hurt you anymore; he's fucking worm food. Even if that douche was still here, I'd never let him put a hand on you again." He wipes my cheek. "Try to get some sleep. Good night."

My core burns as he strides out, but I know it's for the best.

Scarlett

Wake Up

The shower cascades over my body as I lean against the wall. Jackson's words echo in my head. Images of his body against mine send a shiver down my spine. It would be so easy to fall into his arms. Why couldn't I just do *it*? My eyes flutter shut as I slide my hands over my body, imagining Sable is with me. They tweak my nipples and warm their way to my core. I slip a finger inside and move slowly. I bite my lip, wishing his thick digit was there instead.

"Hey, Maya. I left my phone. Do you have any idea where I put it?" I jump as Jackson pops his head around the corner and stares wide-eyed at me. My eyes lock on to his, and I feel like dying of embarrassment. "Well, who needs a phone when you have live action right here?"

"Haven't you ever heard of knocking?"

"Haven't you ever heard of a *vibrator*?"

"GET OUT!" I cover my red face. How could I have been caught *in my own home*? At least he wasn't my dad. "Jackson! I said get out! Don't you dare! Jackson! Get out of my shower!"

His eyes darken as he turns me around and pulls me to him. With my back against his chest, he grabs my shaking hand. "Just pretend I'm not here."

"Like *that* would ever happen."

He grazes my thighs with his fingertips. When I refuse to move, he pushes my finger to my sensitive spot and glides over it. I shiver and throw my head against his broad shoulder. My mouth falls open as he guides my hand in a circular motion. Then, without notice, he removes his touch from mine. "You can do it," he instructs huskily. His erection throbs against my back, as his warmth lingers but never brushes my overheated frame.

"I can't do this with you in here."

"Why not?"

"Because I'm too embarrassed."

"You are a woman with needs," he whispers against my neck. He guides my fingers back into position and starts the magical motions. Just as I'm reaching my breaking point, he stops abruptly. He trails kisses over my neck as his hands finally glide over my hips. "You can do it."

My core throbs with need. He isn't playing fair. I move a shaky hand to my sex, and the whirlwind of desire has me forgetting everything else around me. I gasp as his finger suddenly enters my core and starts dancing deliciously amongst my sweetness. The merciless rhythm of his thick digit helps me reach my climax, and I collapse into his arms while I scream incoherently.

"See? You did it." I can't breathe, let alone throw out my snarky remark. His calloused fingertips glide over my breasts before he begins kneading them. "Do you want me to stop?" he whispers into my ear.

"No," I push out. He pinches my nipple, making me moan in ecstasy. I build up for round two, then he aligns his tip with my core, and I freeze. "Jackson, stop."

"What's the matter?"

"I... I can't do this."

"I am at my breaking point. Please don't do this to me."

"It's just... I feel like I'm betraying Sable's memory by doing *that*."

He gently pushes me away and nods. "It's okay." He slides the bar of soap over my sensitive skin. I whimper softly and lean in to his touch. I hate giving him mixed signals, but I also want to be honest. After he is done washing me, he suds himself up before roughly choking his member. Why is this turning me on? I grab his wrist. "Maya, please, I'm about to burst."

"I know," I stroke him slowly, getting used to his length.

His eyes widen before he drops his head back and thrusts into my palm. "For the love of Luna, go faster." I release his cock and gain his attention. I fall to my knees, my gaze never leaving his perplexed expression. "What are you..."

I collect him in my mouth, and I'm rewarded with a curse as I fit him to the hilt before starting my ruthless assault. Once he is throbbing and thrusting into my throat, I pull away. "*Your* turn," I mock.

He growls, then grabs my hips and thrusts inside me. I scream at the unexpected invasion. "I didn't mean to hurt you." He pulls out slowly.

"No, please, don't stop," I whine as I push my hips against him.

He runs his hand over my back. "Open your eyes." My lashes flutter. "I want you to remember who it was that had you soaring to new heights."

"Promises, promises."

He grins and slips inside me again. This time, teasingly slow, until I'm begging him to pump harder and faster. He obeys, and soon we are both screaming out our release as the cold water cascades around us. "Hey, Maya?"

"Yes?"

"I think we need to take another shower."

My eyes shoot open, and I gasp. I skim my dark room before I fumble for my phone to note the time. "Oh shit. It was only a dream." I suck in air while my lower extremities ache for the visions to be a reality. I groan as I run a hand through my sweaty hair. "I'm not going to survive this cycle, am I?"

"You look like shit." Jackson grins over his mug as I shuffle my feet into my kitchen.

I smooth out my hair. "That's rude."

"You dreamt about me, didn't you?" he whispers.

Thank goodness a knock on the door allows me to ignore him. "Maya, I hope I'm not interrupting anything. I called you last night and left a voicemail. But since I was in the neighborhood, I thought I'd drop in." Debbie hugs me. "Plus, it's always a pleasure to see you."

"*Pleasure,* huh?" Jackson smirks, and I throw him a glare.

"Debbie, I'm sorry I missed your call. What's going on? Is Sara all right?"

"Yes, of course. She's at school. Actually, I wanted to talk to you about the art gallery you are setting up here. Could I enter a few pieces?"

"Oh, yes. I would love to see some of your artwork."

"Perfect. Then I'll bring them by tomorrow."

The way she watches me makes me feel uncomfortable. "Is there anything else you want to talk about?"

"My nephew's girlfriend miscarried the other day."

"Oh no. I'm so sorry, Debbie. Who's your nephew? I will send them a sympathy card."

"Oh, I thought you knew..." Debbie glances at Jackson. "Nobody told her?"

"Frost didn't feel it was necessary."

"Tell me *what*?"

"Oh, dear. Well, you know what? I will just keep my gossip to myself." She stands to leave. "I'll see you tomorrow."

"Wait! Please, Debbie, tell me."

"*Freddy* is my nephew."

"But you're not a shifter, and he is," I blurt out, dumbfounded.

"Remember that story about the Native American and shifter running off? And how they changed the woman's appearance to make it happen? Well, they are part of my bloodline, and now *some* family members possess the ability while most don't. Although I don't have the gene, Freddy's mother does, and she married a shifter."

"So, Freddy is related to you," I reiterate. "And that means *he* was the one who told Spike how to conceal me." I sway before balling my fists. "Did *you* use magic to hide me?"

Debbie steps back with her hands up. "That was *not* me."

"But the tale talks about a spell that changed a shifter, and it was *your* family who conjured it!"

Debbie's head drops. "I'm sorry. Spike threatened my mother, and she submitted to his demands. *Luna, rest her soul.* After you were returned to the pack, Frost came to me demanding answers. And I assumed your parents explained everything to you."

I rub my temples as I absorb her words. Why didn't Debbie tell me sooner? Or Sara? Wait. Why didn't anybody from my *pack* tell me first? I glare at Jackson before backing away from his remorseful stare. "You knew? How could you not tell me?"

"You and Sara are close friends. We didn't want this information to taint that relationship. Especially after everything you have been through," Jackson pleads.

"How could my own pack hide things from me, then pretend it's for my benefit? I have taken care of myself for years. And have dealt with a lot of bullshit, including that scumbag Freddy, even when Sable and I found out he got Sky pregnant and…" I blink. "Oh no. Does that mean *Sky* lost her baby?"

"Yes, dear, I'm so sorry."

As angry as I am that everybody kept this from me, my heart breaks as I realize my little nephew is gone. "But why didn't she tell me?"

"Oh, sweetie, it just happened and, well… Sky is beside herself with grief."

"Of course she is." I stand. "I'll visit her and give her a shoulder to cry on."

Debbie gently grabs my wrist. "Just say a prayer for her, honey. That's all she needs."

"Oh, yes, of course. I'm sure she wants her space right now."

Debbie hugs me. "I'm sorry to be the bearer of bad news. I'll see you tomorrow."

I squeeze her before she walks out. Then I turn an icy glare on Jackson, who backs up. "I was only doing what Frost instructed."

"What else have you done because my dad *instructed* it? Be my friend? Try to sleep with me? Don't come near me." I swipe at my eyes. "You were the one person I had left who I thought I could trust. You've really disappointed me." I stomp to my parents' house and barge in.

"Maya, come on in, dear," Mom sings.

"Did you know about Freddy's involvement with my capture?"

"Honey, why don't you sit down. I'll grab you a bowl of soup. I'll get one for Jackson too."

"I told him to stay away from me. Do I need to ask you and Dad to do the same?"

"Maya, Freddy explained the situation before pleading for forgiveness and a second chance."

"So, that's it? After everything he did?"

"He was forced by Spike, just like you were. And we never consulted you, because we know how upsetting those memories are."

I turn on my heels and stalk off. How could they have knowingly allowed Freddy into our pack with open arms? He was the one who made it possible for Spike to conceal me all these years. And yet, he is a member of our family *and* with Sky. I rub my temples and wonder if Sky knows who she's sleeping with. But I don't have time to worry about that right now, because I have an art gallery to set up.

Scarlett

Final Offering

"**M**aya, everything is beautiful. You did a wonderful job." Debbie smiles as she walks through the art gallery with me. "And your painting is so… *unique*."

I smirk. "It's something all right."

"Excuse me, ladies, but can I borrow the hostess for a moment." The familiar, irritating voice sounds from behind us.

I glare at Jackson, but the girls walk away with conspiratorial winks. "I have *nothing* to say to you."

"Can't we just leave the past in the past?"

"I don't want to talk about it."

Jackson grabs my hand before he tugs me to him. He wraps his arms around me. "Everything looks amazing. Thank you for putting this together for me."

"It wasn't just for *you*."

"And do you know which masterpiece is my favorite? *You*." He twirls me around, and I blush. "Come on. Smile for me." The corner of my lip twitches. "On second thought, just remain stern." He smirks. "It'll keep the males from pouncing on you. I mean, I smelled you before *I* even arrived." He drags his face against my neck. "Are you sure it's safe for you to be out here during this time of the month?"

There he goes, sticking *his nose* in my business. "I hope you have a good night, Jackson." I wave over to Bridgett. "Oh, look, your whore is here," I whisper for only him to hear.

He frowns at me. "Maya…"

"Bridgett, I see you received my invitation."

"Yes, thank you for thinking of me. I do love Jackson's paintings." She bats her lashes.

"Don't we all? Well, you two have a great night. I need to make my rounds." I swipe the sweat from my brow. At least Jackson will be occupied for most of the evening. The twinkling lights hanging on the trees dance in the background as my finger glides over the wolf charm on my necklace. Sable would have loved this event and seeing everyone all dressed up.

"Maya, how are you, dear?"

"Celeste, I haven't seen you in a while."

"I'm sorry. It's been rough, and I didn't want to burden you with my pain."

"Celeste, that wouldn't have been a burden. I love you and your family. Even if Sable isn't, well, you know."

We hug before she sighs. "I promise I won't be a stranger

anymore."

"Debbie told me about Sky and the baby. I'm so sorry."

"Thank you. We were all thrown off by his passing. And poor Sky is having such a rough time dealing with it. She's so angry…"

"Maybe I could come over and see how she's doing?"

"That's very considerate of you. But Sky isn't very hospitable at the moment." She rubs her neck. "To be honest, honey, she blames you for the child's death. All that stress after Sable's passing. It's not right, of course. But it might be best if you keep your distance from her for a while."

"What? She blames *me*?"

"Don't worry, she will come around, sweetie. Just give her time." Debbie waves Celeste over, and she excuses herself.

My legs have a mind of their own as they wander to the large oak tree, away from the noise and the lights. My palm scrapes over the fresh tick mark and a tear falls. Poor Sky. I wish I could do something to ease her suffering. "It sure does feel like old times, huh? Debbie told me she let my secret slip… I hope you are mature enough to let it go." Freddy strides past the tree to a dark grove.

I clench my fists, but ease into a calming stance. As much as I don't like the man, he did just lose a child too. "Why didn't you tell me yourself?"

"Why? So you could hate me *more*? And cause more stress to my mate? Maybe kill *another* baby, or heck, why not another husband? I hear Aspen is still on the market." He balls his fists.

"See? This is the Freddy I know: harsh, cruel, and a complete jackass. But you hide it well, don't you? Around everybody else. But you can't fool me."

Surprise flashes across my face as he slams my body against the tree and glares down at me. "You just won't let me have this, will you?" he hisses. "Good. It'll make *this* a lot easier."

I yelp as he jabs at my neck. I shove him off and look at the syringe in his hand. "What did you do?"

"You should have taken Jackson's advice. A female in heat is in high demand these days." My world blurs before I sway, and he catches me. "It looks like you've had too much to drink, sweetie. Why don't I take you somewhere safe?"

"Don't…" My words fall on deaf ears as he tosses me over his shoulder, and I black out.

"Just tell him I brought a female in heat… Yes! But we are on a time crunch."

"Where…?" I pry open my eyes.

"Did you have a nice nap?" My face jolts to the side as he brings his hand across my cheek. "Welcome to your new home."

I have a hard time hiding my panic. I'm in a small cell with five other females. I squint. And they look familiar. It's the hair and eye color. My eyes widen. "They're from Robert's pack! *You* stole them!"

"No, I just hinted as to where they could be found."

"But why?"

"Because they are trying to replicate our abilities."

"Who?" My voice pitches as I finally notice the men and women in starched uniforms.

"Our military higher-ups. Our government."

"But why would you help them hurt your kind?"

"Because after that blood bath at the warehouse, I had to do something to stay out of prison."

"You are a fucking coward. A traitor."

"And you are my *final* offering. A female who can breed immediately." My blood runs cold. No. I can't become some lab rat to be experimented on! "I'll make sure your funeral is as beautiful as your husband's. Now that I'm free from them, I don't have to look over my shoulder."

"Wait. Just tell me this one thing. Did you even love Sky?"

"What I have with Sky is real," he growls.

"She doesn't even know the *real* you." I see a flash of silver before pain rips through my arm. I scream out and fall to the floor. Blood seeps over my dress.

"I just need to make sure your dad doesn't send out a search party." He slices the fabric from my body and waves it in the air. "Goodbye, *Scarlett*," he hisses. "I would stick around to watch the free porn, but I have a party to attend." He bows and laughs maniacally as he strides out. Once the metal door clangs shut, the other girls rush over and help me stand.

"Are you all right?"

I take in their dirty faces. "Robert has been searching for you all. He really misses you."

Hope sparks in their eyes. "Thank you."

"What is this place?"

Before they can answer, the door slams open. "All right, ladies. Move back." A pudgy guard snatches my elbow and drags me out. When a tall woman steps towards him to object to my removal, I shake my head at her, knowing my fellow captives won't be able to fight off these guards on their own. I don't want any more blood spilt. At least, not *theirs*. Mine, on the other hand... well, I plan to put up one hell of a fight.

"Freddy has finally proven himself useful," a man in uniform sneers. "Throw her in with the males. Odds are one of them will do what needs to be done. If not, we can tie her up."

Now's my chance! I attempt to shift and give these idiots a piece of my mind, but I *can't*. I panic. Why can't I grow my fur? "You can't do this!" I shout. "I'm a human being! I have rights!"

"You're a mangey mutt, who needs to be leashed and taught some manners." I'm pulled back, and tape is slapped over my mouth. "There, that's better. There's nothing worse than a bitch with a loud mouth." He grabs my necklace and throws it to the floor, before stomping on it and crushing all the hope I had of surviving this ordeal.

Scarlett

The Final Battle

The guard drags me—kicking—through a dark hallway. Once he opens a heavy metal door, he throws me in. I skid across the floor. My body comes to a stop, and I flop to my back. The bright fluorescent lights blind me, and I have to close my lids. When I open them again, I gasp into the eyes of a dozen unkempt, visibly starved, seemingly desperate male shifters. "The first one to nail her gets an extra portion of grub tonight." The guard's chuckle bounces off the stone walls as he exits.

One of the men reaches for me, and I pinch my eyes shut. When his hand grabs my bruised arm, I squeeze out a tear. "Take a deep breath. This is going to hurt," he warns before he rips off the tape. I scream as it peels back a layer of my lip along with it. Then he tugs my wrists free. "What's your name, sweetheart? What pack do you belong to?" I take a step in the opposite direction, unsure if I can trust them. "It's okay. We aren't going to hurt you," he whispers.

Standing as tall as I can, I declare my name, lacing every syllable with my alpha tone. "I'm Maya Tala."

There are hushed whispers before the group parts to allow a man to step out from the shadows. My confidence wavers as he approaches. When the light enhances his features, I gasp. A sob escapes and I leap into his arms. I guide my hands all over his body until I reach his overgrown beard and sleep-deprived eyes. "Maya? Is that really you?"

"Oh, my Luna! You need to shave that shit off, Sable. You look like a bum."

He embraces me in a tight hug. "The second we get back home, I will. Anything for you, baby." He kisses my cheeks, my nose, and finally lands on my lips. Our kiss is all teeth and tongue as we hungrily devour each other. My knees grow weak. He catches me and holds me like a child. "I can't believe it's you. I wish I could say I'm happy to see you, but I'm not. Not here."

His words sting, but I know what he means. "I'm in your arms again, and that's all that matters."

"They won't let you stay with me forever."

"But I just got you back!" I wail.

"I know."

"What happened to you? We thought you were killed?"

"They attacked me while I was in the stream. Then I woke up in this cell."

I look around at the rest of the men. They have different hair and eye colors. They must be from different packs too. "But why are you all here? Why did they take you?"

"They are trying to build up their army and add a new tactical team," he scoffs.

I rub my arms as I feel hot tears dampen my cheeks. "Freddy did this to me."

His eyes darken. "What? No. He told us he was forced to do Spike's bidding. That he wanted a fresh start."

"Well, he lied."

"Did he drag Sky into this too? Oh no! Did he give them her baby?"

"I'm sorry to be the one to tell you this, Sable… but Sky lost the baby."

"I'm going to crush that fucking fleabag."

"Get in line."

"How did Freddy get you away from the pack?"

"I was in our territory when he grabbed me."

"Weren't you *with* the pack? They should have protected you!"

"Well, the pack was busy looking at this beautiful art gallery that Mom and I set up. And I did have someone watching out for me, but I kind of sent a girl his way to distract him. I know! I know! Don't give me that look. I feel like shit already." I hold up my arm to distract his anger. "And I got a booboo."

He sighs and kisses my wound. "I really wish you hadn't distracted your protector. But I'm sorry that you're hurt."

"Alpha, we should expedite our plans," a tall, dark-haired man suggests to Sable.

Sable nods. "We finally have the last piece of our puzzle, boys." He grins at me. "A distraction."

"Me?"

"Don't worry, I'll explain everything."

"Are you sure about this?"

"Trust me, our plan will work."

I brush a shaky hand over his cheek. "I still can't believe you are alive. There was so much carnage when they attacked you…"

"There wasn't a day that went by where I didn't think about you. The thought of seeing you again is what kept me going. Now, do you remember the plan?" He trails kisses down my neck.

"We pretend we are doing… *it*. Then, when they come to collect me, you guys will attack, break us out, and we will live happily ever after."

"You got it."

"But why does this plan feel flimsy?"

"Have faith in us. We have been waiting for an opportunity like this, and we are more than ready. Trust me, okay? These men have been away from their loved ones for far too long. They are willing to give it their all to return home." My heart aches as I imagine all of the families, who (like me) assumed the abducted shifters were dead. Well, the good news is: if we fail, they won't even realize it. "Guys, keep your eyes and ears open."

"Look at you, barking out orders, Mr. Alpha," I tease. "For somebody who never wanted this position, you are doing a great job leading them."

"They forced the title on me. The only thing I've done is offer my suggestions. I'm not a fucking dictator like some of the other pack leaders." He pulls me towards a cot in the corner of the room, then runs a finger over the gash on my arm. "I'm sorry, my sweet Maya. You never deserved any of this."

I snatch his chin. "And I would do it all over again, if it meant I got to see you."

He swipes at his cheek. "What's been happening at home since I've been gone." I tell him about the missing wolves, his sister losing the baby and blaming me, and the art gallery I executed. "That was very kind of you, to do that for Jackson."

"Why are you saying it like that?"

"Because it was never a secret that your dad's always favored the beta over me. And I assumed the moment I was out of the picture, he would slide right into my place."

"Hey, that's *not* how it happened."

"Really? So, he hasn't tried to claim you?" I purse my lips at the accusation. "I figured. Does that mean he succeeded? Are you with *him* now?"

"Do you honestly think that little of *me*? That only a few months after losing my husband, I would jump in bed with another man?"

"It would be easy, considering your dad had him at your beck and call this whole time, as a bodyguard. He could have put anybody in that position. And to make things worse, that good-for-nothing beta didn't even do a decent job watching over you! Because look where you are!"

I can't believe that—*after all these months apart*—he's looking to fight with me. "I don't want to argue. This is a happy time because we are finally together again."

"So, you and Jackson aren't a thing?"

"No, you idiot. Now shut up and kiss me." I slam my lips against his, stopping his sour mood. It's amazing, having him back by my side. And if I close my eyes, I can almost pretend we are home. I shiver as he nibbles my earlobe. I wrap my legs around him and groan softly.

"We are only supposed to be *pretending* to have sex," he whispers.

"But these hormones are driving me insane." I situate his palm over my heated core. "Please, it's been so long," I purr, grinding my hips against his. I'm rewarded with a soft growl, and I know I've sparked his wolf's interest.

"I want this more than you know. But not *here*. Not now," he begs. "You deserve so much more than this." I whimper as my center throbs. I glide his finger inside me, and he draws in a breath as my moist muscles embrace him. He tugs his hand back and sucks on the digits, tasting me. His eyes darken as his nose tickles my thighs. I arch my back and huff. "You aren't playing fair," he chastises.

"It's not my fault. Blame stupid wolves and their *heat* cycles," I protest. Sable lowers to the floor, then settles on his knees. His hungry gaze takes in my wet apex as he snatches my ankles and tugs me towards him. My surprised gasp is quickly covered with a moan as he savagely laps up my juices. It doesn't take long before I'm spilling over and screaming my release.

The cot creaks as he settles on top of me. "Will that be enough for now? Until I can get us home?"

My breath releases in rasps, as I continue to enjoy the remaining jolts of pleasure. A playful grin graces my face. "What? Are you getting tired in your old age? Afraid you can't perform anymore? Don't worry, I understand." His mouth covers mine, and we entangle ourselves while we fly high. I dig my nails across his back and join him thrust for thrust, enjoying every second I have with him, because we both know the odds of our escape plan working are slim. All too soon, the door slams open, and a guard marches inside to drag me out. Once he unlocks our only exit, the inmates attack him. The guard releases his hold on me to protect himself, creating the perfect opportunity for me to snatch his sidearm and toss it to Sable.

"Handcuff him inside the cell. We are on to phase two," Sable announces. Our hunting skills are put to the test as we make our way through the compound, releasing prisoners and handcuffing guards. "We are almost there." Sable squeezes my palm. As we turn the corner, my jaw drops. Thirty heavily armed soldiers block our only path to freedom. Once they lock eyes with us, they cock their guns.

"This ends now!" one shouts. "Go back to your cells or bleed out at our feet. Either way, you aren't leaving." The man then clutches my arm and tugs. Sable fumbles as he reaches out for me. But he's thrown backwards when a guard kicks him.

"Stop! Don't hurt him," I screech as blood oozes from the corners of his lips.

"Oh, it looks like the little bitch likes what you did to her, mutt!" The soldier chuckles as he throws me back into his comrade's arms. "Who wants dibs? Huh? I mean, if you're going to die anyway, we might as well have our fun first."

I'm glad the guard has found a different target, so the pack members can help Sable to his feet. "You're a monster," I growl.

"You're mistaken. It's your kind who are the monsters." He grabs a fistful of my hair so I'm forced to look into his eyes. "Because if we didn't drug you, you would have killed us already."

"And yet, *you* don't have to shift to become a killer."

"You're damn right." He points the gun at my temple. "I have all the power. So why don't you show me *more* respect?"

I spit in his face. "That's all the *respect* you deserve. You took us from our families. Then you drugged us so we couldn't defend ourselves. Fuck you," I say slowly.

"You will regret that." He swipes at his face, his finger dancing towards the trigger.

So, this is how my tale ends? Defending my family against the real monsters of this world. I'll take it. I lean in to the hot end of his barrel. "What are you waiting for?"

Scarlett

Help!

We are blasted to the floor as the door sails off its hinges and debris flies everywhere. "Now, everyone!" Sable coughs out. "Run!"

I crawl through the dust until I reach his hand. "Can you stand?"

"Go with the others. Get to safety. Hurry."

"My life is meaningless without you." I huddle beside him.

"Stubborn to the bitter end, huh?"

The room electrifies as a familiar scent wafts my way. My head shoots up. "Azure!" When our eyes meet, my heart flips with relief. The Guardian lifts his hands and blue lightning bolts sizzle down around us. The guards twitch wildly before crumbling to the ground. I let out a breath and lean my head on Sable's chest. "Well, it's about damn time you showed up."

Azure's lips pull up before he helps me to my feet. "I caught your scent and knew there would be trouble in your midst. I'm glad I checked it out."

"Sable is injured. Can you help him?" Once we are safe, I embrace the prisoners and tend to their wounds. Then we begin the long trek home. When I notice Azure lingering, I arch a brow at him.

"I'm staying here for the time being. I need to get to the bottom of this operation, so no one else is taken."

"Will you be safe?"

"Yes, and when my job is complete, I will seek you out and update you."

I hug him tight. "Thank you for saving us."

"I'm sorry it took me so long. Your packs must be worried. Return home. I'll see you soon."

The sun warms our backs as we limp through our territory. Cries of joy surround us and we are immediately embraced by our loved ones. Jackson is the first to grab and squeeze the breath out of me. His hands are shaking as they brush over my face. "Damn it, Maya. Pull that shit again and I'll kill you myself."

"You can't have *my* woman anymore. I'm back to stay," Sable grumbles.

The beta blinks as he takes in my mate. Then he smiles wide before giving him a man hug. "Well, I'll be damned! Look who decided to rise from the dead and steal *my* girl!" They pat each other's back, and I can tell whatever beef they had towards each other has melted away.

"She's worth the trip." Sable smiles down at me.

"Now, that's something we can agree on." Jackson pins me between them with a reassuring embrace.

"Oh, my Luna!" My mom blubbers as she pushes through.

My dad hugs me next. "When Freddy came to us with your bloody clothing, we thought the worst had happened."

That name sends fire through my veins. "Dad, where is Freddy?"

"Why?"

"We need to pay that little shit a visit." Everybody quiets as they gather to hear my abduction story. Then, each returned pack member follows suit. We all share one common element: *Freddy*.

I knock on the front door and wait. Phoenix answers it with a gasp. "Celeste, come quickly!"

We get Sable inside and help him to the couch. Celeste turns the corner, reading a stack of papers. "Why are you shouting across the house?" The papers flutter to the ground as her gaze falls on her son. "Am I dreaming? Sable, is that really you?"

"Yes, Mom. But I'm in rough shape. Do you think you can patch me up?" He grins, and she chokes on a sob as they embrace.

"Phoenix, we need to talk to Freddy," Dad demands.

"I believe he is in the room with Sky."

I jump up, but my dad pushes me back down. "Let *me* handle this."

Sable squeezes my palm. I look into his eyes and smile. He doesn't want me to leave his side. And I don't want that either. I know my dad will put that scumbag in his place. "Freddy snuck out the window," My dad growls as he runs out the front door, shifting as he goes. Phoenix follows at his heels.

"What the hell is going on? Frost just barged into my room, and Freddy jumped out my window." Sky falls to her knees, and her lip quivers as she reaches out to touch Sable's arm. "Sable? Oh, Luna! Sable!"

My mate collects his little sister in his arms and lets her cry into his chest, while he strokes her hair. "It's okay, Sky. I'm here."

My emotions spill over my cheeks as I witness their special sibling reunion. I don't understand Sky's tale, but I know that one day she'll spell it out for others to hear. And when that day comes, I'll listen intently. She meets my eyes. "I'm so sorry I blamed you."

"It's okay. I'm sorry you lost the baby." She pulls me into a hug, and together, we cry over the child she will never cradle. No words can express how badly I feel for her loss, so I just let my actions speak volumes. While Celeste patches up Sable, Sky shows us her ultrasounds and photos. It's bittersweet. We are celebrating the return of Sable, but also mourning the loss of our youngest pack member. "You know what? We are going out and getting matching tattoos in memory of your baby and my nephew," I declare.

"A tattoo of what?" Sky asks.

I hold up the ultrasound of his two little feet. "This. It will remind us to always move forward, no matter how muddy life gets."

We leap up from the couch as the front door flies open, and Freddy is tossed at our feet. "Frost, what the hell is wrong with you." Sky kneels next to her mate's groaning form.

"Get away from him," Phoenix demands.

Sky blinks at her father's command before she refocuses on Freddy. "What have you done?"

"I did what I had to, to survive. To be able to stay with you, Sky."

I clench my fists and step towards him. "You had a second chance, and you fucking blew it. You sold out our kind. Betrayed us all."

My dad pulls Freddy up by his shirt before zip-tying his hands behind his back. "Go ahead and shift like this. I'd love to watch your arms dislocate," he hisses in Freddy's ear. "You are going to be under lock and key until the Guardian arrives to deal with you." Then he shoves the fleabag out the door.

"I don't understand. What did Freddy do that was so wrong?" Sky's lips quiver.

"Come sit next to me, sis, and I'll explain everything," Sable soothes.

"Frost just *shoved* Freddy into his trunk and drove off." Aspen rushes into the room but clamps his mouth shut as his eyes fall on his long-lost brother. He hugs Sable. "Forget Freddy! What are you doing here?"

"I was just about to explain everything to Sky. Why don't you join us, brother?" Sable collects me in his lap as his family gathers to hear his heroic tale about our grand escape.

"Are you sure you're ready for this? We can wait a little longer."

"Mom checked my injuries and they are healed. There's no sign of the serum in my blood. So I'm more than ready." Sable takes a deep breath, and I watch him shift for the first time in months. He's shaky on all fours but his tail wags.

"Does yours itch?" Sky rubs her forearm.

"Yeah, a little." I glance at the matching footprints replicated on our skin.

"Come on, slowpokes!" Aspen grins as he shifts mid-leap and chases after his brother. We smirk at each other, then follow their lead. Since the pack members are all back home, the alphas have lifted our travel restrictions. And it's amazing to *not* be under their constant supervision, although I do miss Jackson's presence. And I constantly worry about how he is taking the news of Sable's return. But I look forward to witnessing his tale unfold one day too.

A scent on a nearby pine tree has my ears prickling. My nose stabs the air and I bullet towards the valley. My tongue hangs out as I leap in the air and crash into my target. I lick his face as my tail wags. My pack gasps and steps back, waiting for the Guardian to react. "Maya, thank you for the welcome." Azure strokes my fur.

I shift before rolling off him. "You took forever! Did you find out why they were holding us? Did you read their minds and uncover how deep it went? Are there *more* compounds?"

"That is a lot of questions for me to answer in *one* breath. How about we go see Freddy, and I will explain my findings?"

Sable pulls me to him. "Why are you all over him?" he grumbles. "Give the man some breathing room."

"I read the memories of the guards. They were trying to create an army of shifters for the government, though it seems that this was a localized event. But I don't know for sure. Somehow, they've found a way to weaken my abilities. That's why I didn't know trouble was brewing."

"But *who* authorized the attacks?" Dad prompts.

"I have a lead, a man they call the *General*, but I'm not completely sure who he is. I've contacted the other Guardians, and they're going to investigate in their quadrants, then report back if they find anything amiss."

"What were you able to find out about Freddy's involvement in all of this?" I ask.

"Freddy's situation is complicated. They rode him pretty hard to locate more shifters for their experiments and threatened Sky if he didn't comply. His actions were wrong, but he did them for the survival of his mate and child."

"Is he sorry?" I counter.

"No, Freddy is not remorseful. He considers his actions justified, and I believe he would do it all over again."

"I can't allow him to live amongst my pack anymore. It's not safe," Dad declares.

"I will turn him over to the authorities."

"Can we even *trust* them? After everything?" I question.

"Only time will tell. And I promise I'll be checking in on him often."

"Please, Guardian, stay and celebrate with us. You are our guest of honor tonight."

"I appreciate that. Thank you. Oh, before I forget…" Azure places something on my palm. "I think this is yours."

I open my hand and my eyes tear up. "You found my necklace." I clasp the chain and watch it sparkle against my chest. "Now, it's exactly where it belongs."

Jackson hands me a wrapped canvas. I take it and smirk. "Is it my birthday again already?" I unravel the paintings and my jaw drops as I flip through them. The first one is of my mom, my dad, and me when I was a baby. The second is the one of Sable and me on our wedding day. But the third brings tears to my eyes. It's a portrait of me laughing at one of Jackson's dumb jokes. I run my hand over my face. I've never look this beautiful. "Jackson…"

"I know they aren't perfect, but I thought you would like them."

"They are unbelievable. When did you do this last one?"

"When I thought we lost you." He runs his hand down my cheek. "I will always cherish the moments we shared. Thank you." Sable clears his throat, and Jackson smirks. "The next time this guy decides to die, I'll make sure to close the deal a lot faster. I won't waste time."

Sable narrows his eyes. "I'll give you a five-second head start… before I rip your throat out."

The beta precariously pops a kiss against my lips, then runs. My mate's eyes grow wide, and he dashes after him. My mom wraps an arm around me and sighs. "Ah, young love."

I laugh as I watch them wrestle in the grassy field. "It's an unfair fight. My poor husband is still recovering from his time in captivity. Should I break them up?" I frown as Jackson pins Sable.

"Hmm, let me watch a little longer, dear."

"Mom, you and Dad should have this. Jackson made it for you, after all." I hand her the painting of our family. She takes it and runs her fingertips over the brushstrokes.

"Thank you, sweetheart." She hugs me. "Has Sable picked up on any of your changes yet?"

"Not yet."

"He will be so happy when he finds out."

"Then I guess I should save him from Jackson, or our child may be fatherless." I yelp as my dad lifts me into a hug.

"Did I hear correctly? I'm going to be a grandfather!" His happiness washes over me, bringing tears to my eyes. Then he takes off towards Sable and Jackson's dog pile. They all wrestle around like pups until the sun sinks low over the horizon.

Scarlett

Happily Ever After

"Thank you all for joining our celebration as we welcome back our pack members who were taken. We praise Luna for her protection over our loved ones during their time in captivity. And we honor our Guardian, who stepped in just in time to save them. Please, everybody, raise your glass. To Azure, Luna's mighty protector."

"To Azure!" We all clap before chatting amongst each other in the large field, a fire blazing in the center. I'm mesmerized as the flames crackle and shoot sparks of gold into the clear night sky.

"I thought you were going to tell *me* before anybody else?" Sable hands me a bottle of water.

"My mother guessed, and I only confirmed her suspicions. Then my dad, with his large wolf ears, heard everything. Are you disappointed, Sable? I know we had a five-year plan, and I wanted to be working."

"I'm the happiest I've ever been, Maya. Thank you." Sable kisses me tenderly as he guides his hand over my belly. I lean my head on his chest and listen to his strong heartbeat. I'm blessed to have a second chance with my mate. Then I see Jackson dancing around the fire. I hope he can find someone to settle down with again.

"Maya, congratulations," Sky offers before walking over.

I can tell by the look in her eyes that the statement stings her heart. I bite my lip. I never considered how much this pregnancy news would hurt her. "Sky, I'm so sorry..."

"Silly! Don't be sorry! This is a great gift!" She hugs me tight. "And I will be the best aunt ever." We turn as we hear someone clear their throat.

"Azure, are you enjoying your party?"

"Yes, thank you. I heard congratulations are in order."

"Thank you. Have you met Sky yet?"

Sky takes a step back from Azure's towering frame. The Guardian frowns at her reaction but extends a hand in greeting. She shakes it and forces a smile. "It's nice to meet you." She turns to me. "I should go check on Aspen. He was hitting on Robert's daughter, last I saw him." I watch her leave with slumped shoulders.

"Sable, I'm worried about your sister."

"She's strong, but we'll watch over her."

I pivot to ask the Guardian's opinion, but he isn't paying attention to our conversation anymore—his gaze follows Sky's departing figure. "Are you okay, Azure?"

He blinks and turns to me. "It has been a long time since I was amongst a pack. It feels awkward and comforting at the same time. If that makes sense."

"That was how I felt when I first arrived here too." I wrap my arms around Sable. "But I have no regrets with how things turned out for me. I finally found my happily ever after."

Epilogue

"**B**rian! Get your butt back here, you little—and there he goes." I toss down the diaper as I watch his furry butt take off.

"Stop worrying. He'll be fine, Maya."

I shove a finger in Sable's chest. "Then *you* hunt him down for his checkup."

"Oh, is that today? Whoops."

"Yes, and now I have to get him out the door, with clothes on, in less than an hour. How other shifters deal with their children is beyond me. I thought Sara was bad, but this sure takes the cake."

Sable kisses my head. "I love you. I'll get your dad to wrangle him up. And if that doesn't work, I'll use Jackson as bait and let Brian attack him. Besides, shouldn't you be somewhere?" I tilt my head in thought. *Where am I supposed to be?* This whole motherhood brain sucks. "Today is your first day at St. Paul's Orphanage."

"Shit!" I stomp around, collecting my teaching supplies before throwing my bag over my shoulder. "I never should have signed up for this."

"Hey, you are a great teacher, with a heart of gold. Plus, you love volunteering over there."

"Volunteering and working are two very different things, Sable," I lecture as I walk out the front door.

"Hey! You forgot something!"

I turn on my heels while I scan the cluttered living room. "What?"

Sable grins and wraps his arms around my waist. "My goodbye kiss." I peck him on the cheek, *so* not in the mood for his cutesy stuff right now, especially when I'm already running late. "Hey, cheapo!" He collects me in his arms, and I melt as he kisses me deeply while his hands ravage my body.

"This doesn't even begin to excuse your behavior for letting Brian run off."

"I promise he'll make it to his appointment."

"And what about the shop?"

"I'll take him with me again. If he gets to be too much, Mom will watch him for a while. Don't worry. Go."

We both turn as growling and footsteps approach. "I think this beast belongs to you, Sable." Jackson shoves Brian forward. Then he looks me over. "Well, somebody forgot to brush her hair this morning. Sable slacking off on his parenting duties... *again*? Do you need me to pick up the slack?" Jackson drapes an arm around my neck and grins.

"I don't have time for this, Jackson. I'm late."

"I can *ride* you to the orphanage." He smirks. "I mean *drive* you. You can brush your hair on the way."

Sable and Brian both snarl. "There's too much testosterone in here. Goodbye, everybody." I kiss Brian on the head and Sable on the cheek.

"What about me?" Jackson pouts. I flip him the bird as I jog to my car. Then, over my shoulder, I see my husband and son pouncing on the smart-mouthed beta. They will never learn.

"Maya! We are going to be late!"

"I'm sorry, Sara. I lost track of time trying to wrestle with Brian. He has another round of shots today."

I toss her my keys. "You drive. That way, I can brush my hair."

"Really?"

"You have your learner's permit now. Why not?" Her eyes light up as she settles into the driver's seat. Her hands smooth over the steering wheel. "Seat belt, please," I remind her.

Once she buckles up, she turns to me with a pout. "Please, please, please. Can we drive with the top down?"

"But my hair!" I screech.

"It looks great the way it is."

"You are a dirty, filthy liar. It's a rat's nest. I probably have a surplus of cereal in there." I run my hand through my hair. It gets stuck in a knot, and sure enough, a cheerio falls out. I pinch it between my fingers and shove it in her face. "See!" Her laugh is heartwarming, and soon we are both giggling. "Fine. Put the top down."

"You are the absolute best." I shake my head in response as she takes off towards the highway, but then turns on a side street. "I just want to make a quick stop," she adds.

"We are running late!"

"*Please.* I promise I will wash your car free for a month."

Her negotiation raises my eyebrow. "Fine."

"Yes!"

We pull up to the Canis family home, and she holds down the horn. Aspen pokes his face out the front door with a frown. He walks over and shakes his head. "I can't believe you trust a teenager to drive your car. That's asking for trouble."

"Shut up. Not everybody is a bad driver like you." Sarah sticks her hand out. "Pay up, wolfman."

Aspen groans, fishes for his wallet, and passes a twenty-dollar bill to Sara. Then he leans over the side. "Did you still need help with your algebra?"

"Yes, Debbie is on my butt to get a tutor." Sara rolls her eyes.

Aspen snatches the twenty back with a grin. "Come by tonight with your math book."

"Hey! I would rather have the cash!"

"No, you need to pass your final. I'll use it to buy us pizza. Deal?"

Sara looks him over and sighs. "Fine. But you better give me my money's worth. And make sure you get my favorite toppings. No anchovies, fur ball."

"Hey, you ate it just fine last time, without complaint, two-legs. Don't be late."

"See you tonight. Good luck today, Maya."

We watch him close the door before I turn to Sara. "Aspen is ten years older than you."

"I'm well aware of his age."

Luna, help me. Why do I feel like I'm raising a pack of children all of a sudden?

Sara whoops for joy as the car hits the highway. She shoots me a grin before slamming the gas petal to merge into the next lane.

My life is certainly blessed, even if I'm late for my first day, with cheerios stowed in my hair.

Acknowledgments

This book baby never would have been born without the many individuals who breathed life into its pages.

First and foremost, I want to thank my husband, who supports me financially and emotionally. You are my rock, baby! Thank you for all your hard work, tool vocabulary, "permission" to write dirty scenes, and this wonderful cover design. I'll never forget the many hours I watched you tweak a man's crotch so it would look just right.

To my children (who I'm sure are now embarrassed), thank you for sharing your imaginations and feedback with me so I could develop the shifter world. Paul, thank you for insisting I insert a guardian angel type character with superpowers and drawing many illustrations to help push the tale forward. Charles, thank you for suggesting that the fantasy world should have a "contemporary feel" to it, so it's more tangible for my readers.

A huge shoutout to my editor, Kat Pagan! She is a word witch, and without her amazing techniques, this book wouldn't be as awesome as it is! Thank you for your hard work and dedication! I'm so blessed!

Also, a super-sized thank you to all my beta and arc readers! You guys are amazing! The fact that you took time out of your already crazy schedules to read and answer feedback blows me away! I couldn't have done it without you! Especially Frankie, for her help with formatting and her input on my first ever dual POV narrative. Courtney, for her encouraging feedback on my first ever written sex scene. Alicia, for the reminder that not all amazing characters should be named Jeremy, as well as for the name change suggestion: Jackson. And Becky, for introducing me to the comic *Wolf Children*.

Finally, thank **YOU**! Without readers, I couldn't continue my writing dreams.

Additional Titles by the Author

Feathered Dreams Series (a rags-to-riches, clean romance):

Join Ann and be swept into a world of swoon-worthy characters, glittering gowns, and unrelenting intrigue.

Ann is beginning to see how naïve she has been, though by no fault of her own. Farming side by side with her father, away from the drama of the outside world, is what she has always loved most. But now that she is at the Palace, she is forced to focus on other people and their daily struggles. In the midst of her personal growth, she starts to realize how cruel the world can be. Will she shy away and run back to the familiarity of her old life? Or can she share her unique sense of compassion and fierce loyalty to help those in need?

Feathered Dreams (Book 1)

Plucked (Book 2)

Molting (Book 3)

Split Feather (Book 4) TBA 2022

To Be Titled (Book 5) TBA 2023

Wolves of Cold Creek (18+, paranormal romance):

The Cold Creek packs are loyal—while bursting with mouthwatering, unclaimed shifters—all just waiting for their mates. Why not drop in and enjoy the picturesque views by day and scorching fires at night? Don't be shy. They don't bite… hard.

Scarlett's Tail (Scarlett and Sable)

Sky's Tail (Sky and Freddy) TBA 2023

About the Author

Brittany Putzer is a stay-at-home multitasker, living in Florida with her husband, two sons, and mini zoo. She turns to books to escape the world because it's easier to pretend to be a shifter, princess, wizard, vampire, or damsel in need of an alpha. Although she enjoys reading, her passion is writing. And in 2020, she published her first book: *Feathered Dreams*. Her writing style is a creative blend of dark and light themes, sprinkled with sarcasm, humor, romance, and intrigue.

Scan the QR code to chat with Brittany on social media, **review** her books, get signed paperbacks, check out merchandise, and join her newsletter for freebies and sneak peeks.

www.ingramcontent.com/pod-product-compliance
Lightning Source LLC
Chambersburg PA
CBHW052031260626
47163CB00005B/130